Puffin Books
Editor: Kaye Webb

Septimus and the M

'You dreamed it,' said the Reverend Septimus Treloar
severely.

Alisdair shook his head violently so that his lank hair
whipped like a flywhisk. 'I didn't, Septimus. Honest,
I didn't. It all happened, just like I said.' And indeed
how could anyone have dreamed the terrifying things
he had seen and heard when he went to investigate
the sounds of organ music in the Minster church,
that sudden horrible flaring of light, the appalling
dissonant chord on the organ, the darkness and
silence that followed, and the sudden fearful human
scream, rising to such a pitch that it made the
glass tremble beneath his cheek?

After that Septimus was so busy about his parish that
he almost forgot Alisdair's story – until the gossip
started circulating in the town about the ghost of a
murdered Minster organist, and the Dean asked him
to try and solve the mystery before the press got on to
it.

This complicated and exciting story with its ex-
detective hero is a worthy successor to Stephen
Chance's other Puffin, *Septimus and the Danedyke
Mystery*.

For readers of ten and over.

Stephen Chance

Septimus and the
Minster Ghost

Puffin Books
in association with The Bodley Head

Puffin Books: a Division of Penguin Books Ltd,
Harmondsworth, Middlesex, England
Penguin Books Australia Ltd, Ringwood,
Victoria, Australia
Penguin Books Canada Ltd, 41 Steelcase Road West,
Markham, Ontario, Canada
Penguin Books (N.Z.) Ltd, 182–190 Wairau Road,
Auckland 10, New Zealand

First published by The Bodley Head 1972
Published in Puffin Books 1974

Copyright © Stephen Chance, 1972

Made and printed in Great Britain by
Cox & Wyman Ltd, London, Reading and Fakenham
Set in Linotype Pilgrim

Contents

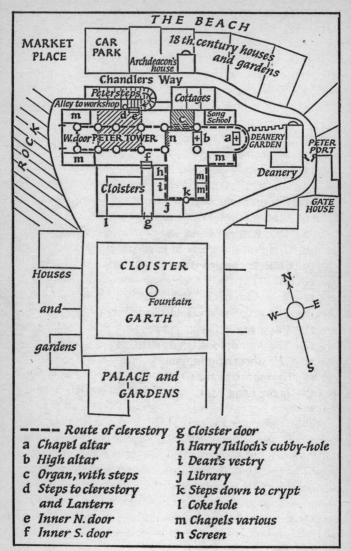

Minster Saint Peter

1 Music out of the Air

It started with Alisdair Cameron, the Dean's son, and the light he saw through the east window of the Minster at one o'clock in the morning. But until long after the ghost had hit the national papers, the only person who knew that was the Reverend Septimus Treloar. Alisdair told him because he was a friend, and because – before he had become a country parson – he had been a Chief Inspector in the C.I.D. Alisdair did not tell his father because he was not supposed to climb out of his bedroom window, especially not at one o'clock in the morning.

It was the first day of the summer holidays, and Alisdair was home from school in his own bedroom with its wide, mock-gothic window which was dominated by the great east end of the Minster, and which gave a view to the left of the green square of Cloister Garth, and to the right a panorama of Minster Saint Peter, its market-place, its harbour, and the ships riding in the treacherous approach from the North Sea.

Alisdair did not sleep well. He never did on the first night home. His own bed was so much softer than the one in the dormitory of the Queen's School. He read until quite late, savouring the freedom to do so. He started a fourth reading of Conan Doyle's *Hound of the Baskervilles*. Alisdair was a lover of detective fiction in general, and of Sherlock Holmes in particular. Soon he was deep in the wild tale of Holmes and Watson and strange doings on Dartmoor.

'I ... counsel you by way of caution to forbear from crossing the moor in those dark hours when the powers of evil are exalted.'

With a tingle of mystery to come, and a warm glow at the thought of the summer holidays stretching away into the misty distances of autumn, Alisdair yawned, put down his book and switched off the bedside lamp.

So he slept.

It was the clock in the Petertower chiming one which woke him. He lay in the warmth, enjoying the comfort of his bed and the glorious knowledge that he need not get up at half past seven in the morning; that there would be no lessons; that he would be able to wear what he liked and do what he liked. It was then that he heard the Minster organ start to play. Only for a few seconds, and he did not hear it very clearly. But he was absolutely certain it was the organ because the top pane of his window – the one that opened on to the top of the garden wall – started to rattle as it always did when Mr Berwick, the organist, did things with his feet and the thirty-two-foot pipes. Alisdair rolled over and propped himself on his elbow, listening in the darkness. Now there was only the ticking of his alarm clock and a hunting owl going home to the elm tree in the Archdeacon's garden. But it *had* been the organ. And it *was* one o'clock in the morning. On impulse he slid out of bed, slipped a sweater over his pyjamas and ran to the window.

There was no moon, but after the darkness of the bedroom it seemed light outside. To his right, over the fake battlements of the garden wall, were the lights of the town. He opened the window and stuck out his head. The night air was cold. Beyond the town the pavilion on the pier was still brightly lit. Faintly the sound of dance music came from it. Green and red, the navigation lights of a ship twinkled just beyond the harbour bar. In front of him loomed the great bulk of the Minster, black against the sky. And at the top of the Petertower, yellow and serene, the light in the Lantern shone out, proclaiming, as it had done for five hundred years, a safe landfall and a snug harbour for mariners.

He pushed the window wide and stepped out on to the wall. On his right the battlements gave some protection from the drop into Chandlers Way. On his left the Deanery garden was blurred and indistinct. The stone of the walkway was like dry ice to his bare feet, and he ran along the wall until it ended just below the east window of the Minster. He scrambled up the sloping sill of the great window and put his eye to the one, well-remembered clear pane in the stained glass picture of Saint Peter in his boat.

At first there was nothing to see. Nothing to hear. Only the vague brightness which was the west window, infinitely remote, down the cavern of the nave. In sound, only the murmurs of the sleeping town.

But then there was something! At first only a blur, a brightness, high up, just below the clerestory windows along the north wall. A point of light and a flicker – as if someone struck a match in the far, far distance on the moors on a black night. It was difficult to see through the small pane of glass, for it was thick and it distorted vision. But there was a light, and it was moving slowly along the wall, becoming better defined as it moved. There was a pinpoint of brightness surrounded by a glow, and it was throwing shadows across the great pillars of the nave and across the clerestory windows as it moved steadily eastward. It was a lamp or a lantern. Someone was walking down the clerestory. Suddenly Alisdair could see the balustrade which guarded the clerestory walkway. It appeared as a sharp black line in the light of the lantern, and behind it there was a dark figure outlined against one of the windows.

Figure and lantern disappeared behind the organ, and for

a moment he saw in silhouette the great pipes like battlements, and the triumphant angels which crowned the instrument. Then the light went out and all was black.

For a long half minute Alisdair remained lying across the cold stone of the sill, his eye pressed to the window, gazing into the darkness. He was just about to get up when suddenly, like the last flicker of a dying fire, the light flared up again, and there was an appalling dissonant chord on the organ. Then darkness and silence. But out of the darkness and the silence there came a scream, a human scream, rising to such an unearthly pitch that it made the glass tremble beneath Alisdair's cheek. As it died away into nothingness, so Alisdair turned and ran – blindly, dangerously – along the top of the wall. He slammed the bedroom window behind him, paused a moment – conscious of his own trembling – and then put on the light. He found a big vase and placed it on the sill so that it must be knocked over if the window were opened. He closed the curtains and opened his bedroom door and looked down the landing to assure himself of the solidity of his father's door and the short distance to it. So he climbed back into bed, and gradually his trembling stopped. But he did not sleep until dawn was lightening the mellow stone of the east end of the Minster.

The Reverend Septimus Treloar switched off the motor mower, wiped his hands on a rag and then wiped the sweat from his face with the same rag, thereby streaking his forehead with oil. Not that anybody except perhaps his mother would have thought that the smears detracted much from his beauty. His face really looked as if someone had tried to remodel it with a baseball bat. Apart from shrewd eyes of a surprising blue, he looked more like a failed prize fighter than anything else.

It was half past twelve, and it was hot. Septimus had

spent all morning mowing the churchyard. He had had enough of it, and he had a thirst like a brewer's drayman's. He left the mower where it was, whistled up his dog, a Great Dane puppy called Grace, who was very sensibly asleep in the shadow of a tombstone, and went across the road to the Bluebell.

He passed the time of day with Charlie, the landlord, made the usual comments about the weather and the visitors, and then took his usual pint of bitter and meat pie out of the bar into the little garden. He sat in the sunshine, his dog on her side at his feet, enjoying sunshine and beer and pie, nodding to parishioners passing down the sleepy village street. As he looked over the low wall he saw a boy on a bicycle come from the direction of the main road. The boy was cycling fast, as if he was in a race, his head down over the handlebars. He suddenly stuck out an arm and turned abruptly up the pot-holed Rectory drive.

'Oy!' bellowed Septimus. 'Alisdair! I'm over here. Outside the pub.'

The bellow startled Grace, bringing her leaping to her feet and barking as if she had failed in her duty.

Septimus growled at the dog so that she subsided like a pricked football, while the bicycle described a tight loop between the Rectory gateposts. Alisdair propped the bicycle against the post of the pub sign and came through the gate into the garden while Septimus leaned sideways and shouted into the cool, dark bar.

'Charlie! Another pie and a bottle of pop. Yes, I did say pop. Hullo, Watson! Written any good murder mysteries lately? And what brings you out to the wuthering wilds of Danedyke Saint Mary's?'

'I've got a case for you, Holmes,' said Alisdair without further greeting, and started to tell his story of the previous night.

Septimus listened without interruption, his eyes half closed, one hand on Grace's head, the other playing with his tankard.

He was fond of young Alisdair, and there was a queer friendship between them, born perhaps of a common loneliness. Septimus was unmarried and lived alone in his inconvenient Rectory. Alisdair was an only child whose mother had died two years previously. When they had first met, Alisdair, quoting the Sherlock Holmes stories, had made a sly remark about the 'official police'. Septimus had caught the reference and pointed out that now he was no longer with Scotland Yard he was a 'consulting detective'. So the friendship between them had begun. Often now they called one another Holmes and Watson, largely because Alisdair had threatened to write an account of Septimus's rackety life.

When Alisdair had finished his story, Septimus remained silent for a moment, trying to think himself into the situation.

'This light,' he said, 'it was swaying?'

'Yes. Like someone carrying a lantern.'

'A torch?'

'No. There was no beam. It was like a lantern.'

'An electric lantern – like the one I carry in the land-rover?'

'Could be.'

Septimus screwed up his face, calling to mind the layout of the Minster.

'And it came along the clerestory walkway, along the north wall? From where the circular stairs go up from the top of the Petersteps, right along to the organ?'

'Yes. That's right.'

'As if someone came up the Petersteps from the market, and then up the circular stairs?'

'Yes. Only you know as well as I do that Tulloch always locks the door at the bottom of the Petersteps after evensong. And they never unlock the circular stair door except when they want to go up to the Lantern. Mostly, the only way up is by the steps to the organ loft.'

Septimus nodded. The Minster was built on a rock commanding the harbour. From the north where the market lay, it was approached by a steep and famous covered stairway called the Petersteps. At the top of the Petersteps, before you actually went through the door into the Minster, on your right there was an insignificant arched door which gave on to a circular stairway. Fifty-seven stone steps took you to another door leading out on to the clerestory walkway. A further one hundred and twenty-seven brought you to the Lantern at the very top of the Petertower.

Septimus ruminated, his eyes closed now, not noticing that Grace was licking his hand preparatory to stealing the remains of his meat pie. Organ music. A shadowy figure with a lantern. A scream out of the darkness. It was an odd story. An odd story from a nervy boy with a vivid imagination. A boy with no brothers or sisters, whose mother was dead, and whose father was a charming, saintly and remote scholar.

He opened his eyes and gazed severely at Alisdair, not noticing the loss of the remains of his lunch.

'You dreamed it.'

Alisdair shook his head violently so that his lank hair whipped like a fly whisk.

'I didn't, Septimus. Honest, I didn't. It all happened, just like I said.'

'Umm,' said Septimus. 'Why haven't you told your father?'

Alisdair was scornful. 'Climbing out of my bedroom window? At one o'clock in the morning? You must be joking. He'd crown me with the Early Fathers in folio.'

Septimus nodded. It was a sound argument.

'Sorry to sound disbelieving,' he said. 'Coppers are a shocking mistrustful lot, Alisdair. Always wondering why people are lying. Don't suppose I shall ever get out of the habit. Anyway, Watson, I'll think about it a bit. What are you doing this afternoon?'

'Nothing much.'

'Well, I'm taking a twelve bore up to the warren on the Home Farm. Bag a bunny for the pot. Like to come?' He had been planning no such thing. Really he had been intending to spend the time mowing the churchyard, but now it seemed a very good idea.

They spent a happy, sunlit afternoon crawling about in the bracken and came back to the Rectory as the sun was beginning to slant down into the west. They were both muddy, tired and contented, and they had four rabbits – one of which Alisdair had shot.

Alisdair was so proud of his expertise, and so aware of the bruise on his collar bone from not holding the twelve bore tight enough that he seemed to have forgotten the mysterious music and light in the Minster.

Septimus gave him two of the rabbits.

'Give 'em to Mrs Wedge,' he said. 'One of them's yours, anyway.'

Mrs Wedge was the Deanery housekeeper.

Alisdair thanked him, climbed on to the bicycle, paused a moment and then looked up at the big priest.

'Well, Holmes, what about the case?'

'Two things,' said Septimus. 'One: I shall ring Harry Tulloch ... Oh, don't worry! I shall only tell him I've "received information". See if he's noticed anything. Ask him to make sure his locks are O.K. Second thing – somewhere or other, and I don't remember where, Sherlock says it is a cardinal error to theorize ahead of your facts. We haven't enough to go on, so I shan't do anything yet. But you keep your eyes open, my lad, and tell me right smartish if anything more happens.'

Alisdair nodded, said good night and cycled away down the drive. Suddenly, just as Septimus was turning into the Rectory front door, he made a skidding turn on the bicycle and came cycling back.

'Holmes,' he said, 'remember *The Dancing Men?*'

'Yes,' said Septimus, wondering what was coming.

'There wasn't enough to go on in that case. And when there was enough – it was too late. Poor old Thingy was dead.' Alisdair said no more. He had made his point and he cycled off down the drive in a vague atmosphere of disapproval, two dead rabbits swinging from his handlebars.

Septimus went back into the house and rang the head verger, Harry Tulloch. Harry was a pal of his; they had served together in the War. So Harry was glad to chat to his old commanding officer. But he had nothing to add to Alisdair's story. Indeed, he transparently thought the whole thing was nonsense. He was quite confident of his own locks, absolutely sure of his security precautions. However, he did promise to keep his eyes and ears open and to ring Septimus if anything out of the ordinary happened. And with that Septimus had to remain content.

2   Before 1935

Nothing happened for a month, and in the busy round of his country parish Septimus almost forgot about Alisdair Cameron's story. Then one evening he returned from a hospital visit to Wisbech to find a note wound into the top of his typewriter. It was written by Mary Crowle, the headmistress of the village school. She and Rosemary Barton, the churchwarden's wife, had been duplicating the parish magazine on the antiquated machine in the corner of the study.

'Will you please ring Mr Tulloch at the Minster in the morning? Mary.'

Next morning Septimus waited until matins in the Minster would be safely over, and then rang the cathedral number. He could hear the 'burr-burr' of the ringing tone as he waited, imagining Harry coming out of his cluttered cubby-hole where he was probably making a cup of tea with Ted Barnes, the assistant verger. The phone was in the Dean's vestry, next door. Harry would be saying unverger-like things under his breath. He had been an ordnance sergeant, learned in the ways of violent death, before he became a verger.

'Minster Saint Peter. Mr Tulloch, head verger, speaking.' Septimus winked down at Grace, whose head was on his knee. Harry always talked like that, making it sound as if he was butler to God Himself. But Septimus knew Harry's harum-scarum past.

'Harry . . . Septimus here. Septimus Treloar. You asked me to ring.'

'Ah. Good morning, Major. I'm glad you're out of bed – as the actress said to the bishop.' Septimus grinned. God's butler had given place to the ordnance sergeant.

'Now then, Tulloch, I'll have you remember you're talking to a member of the Cloth. And what can I do for you, you horrible apology for an ex-soldier?'

Harry suddenly sounded serious.

'Major. You phoned me – five weeks ago – about goings-on in the Minster.'

'You've seen something?'

'Yes. And there's talk in the town, and I don't like it, Major. Lights and the organ, and a crazy old biddy that keeps a bookshop just off the market. Talking about haunting, she is. And there's the Archdeacon – well, you know the Archdeacon, Major. Least said soonest mended. On about thermometers, he is. My locks are still on top line. Checked 'em again yesterday. But . . . well, I'd like to have a chat, Major, and that's the honest truth.'

Septimus digested this, the telephone receiver in one hand, the other on Grace's head. So it was not only Alisdair Cameron. Harry and Ted had seen things. There was talk in the town. And the Archdeacon was interested . . . well, the Archdeacon was an expert on spiritualism and extra-sensory-perception. What time he could spare from arch-deaconing he spent demolishing ghosts and mediums. A possible newspaper headline floated into Septimus's mind, 'Ghost Walks in Haunted Minster'. The Dean would not like that.

'Are you still there, Major?'

'Yes, Harry. Just thinking. Look, I'm "duty dog" on Monday. Can it wait till then?'

'Don't see why not,' said Harry. 'See you Monday, sir.'

Septimus rang off. During the high tourist season the country clergy of the diocese took it in turns to be on duty in the Minster to show visitors round. The job came up once a month, and the following Monday happened to be Septimus's turn.

Septimus put down his cup of coffee and watched Harry Tulloch polishing a silver chalice with his thumb. They were sitting together in Harry's cubby-hole next to the Dean's vestry. The cubby-hole was a tiny vaulted room cluttered with candlesticks, vases, pieces from the Easter garden and figures from the Christmas crib awaiting repair. It smelt of metal polish, candlegrease, incense and communion wine.

'So you see, Major, there's not a lot to go on – nothing really solid, as you used to say in the old days. But it's odd – distinctly odd, as the bishop said to the actress. I heard it one night – the organ playing when it didn't ought to have been. I knocked up Ted Barnes, and he heard it too. We reckoned we saw a light – though we couldn't be sure. So we unlocked. But when we got in there wasn't anything. No light. No organ. Nothing at all.'

'What time?' asked Septimus.

'Oh! Round about one.'

'And which way did you go in?'

'We went up and round,' said Harry. 'Through the Peterport and in through the cloisters and the south door. You know where I live, Major, in the Cottages – in Chandlers Way? Well, it's quicker to go up the hill and in by the south door than down the hill and in by the Petersteps. Ted lives next door to me. He always says it's the steps as makes the difference.'

'So by the time you got round and in at the south side,' said Septimus, 'a villain could have scarpered down the Petersteps and out into the market-place without you knowing?'

Harry looked at him scornfully. 'He'd have to have a key wouldn't he now?'

'And who has got keys?'

'Well of course I have. And Ted. And the Dean and the Archdeacon. Mr Berwick of course – and the precentor ... Blimey! There's a hell of a lot of 'em when you come to add it up.'

'And of course you keep yours there,' Septimus pointed to the keyboard over his head, 'where any stray layabout could put a sticky hand in. Make a wax impression in three seconds flat – as you well know, Harry Tulloch.'

He shook his head mournfully, only half playfully. 'Thought I taught you better than that Harry, really I did.'

Harry was both aggrieved and ashamed. 'Well ... you don't expect to have to think about security. Not seriously like. After all, it is a cathedral, not a bloody weapons establishment.'

'What about this old biddy that keeps the bookshop?' asked Septimus changing the subject.

'Ah. That was the night before I rang you. Made me ring you really. Fair put the frighteners on me, she did. I was down in the Master Mariner having a drink with Ted. She was there with a gin big as a goldfish bowl in front of her. She mostly is, come to that. She butted in on Ted and me talking. Fat as Croesus. Name of Ma Wenlock. She'd heard the organ, so she said, and seen lights going down by the clerestory. And more than once. Haunted she says it is, by the ghost of an eighteenth-century organist. Ted knew her. He said she'd been a spiritualist, or a medium or somesuch ...' Harry paused, holding the gleaming chalice to the dim, unshaded bulb in the middle of his cubby-hole, squinting at it with one professional eye. 'Only the thing was, Major ... fair made my blood run cold it did ... she had such a way of telling her damn silly tale that all the saloon bar was listening. "Cripes!" I thought. "We'll have a rumour of haunting all over the bleeding town. Have it in the papers. The Dean'll do his flippin' nut".'

When he had finished his stint as 'duty dog' and ushered the last tourist out of the Minster, with a great sigh of relief Septimus took off his cassock and hurled it incontinently into Harry Tulloch's cubby-hole. Thankfully he stepped out into cloister Garth where the evening sun and the great square of beautifully tended grass and the surrounding eighteenth-century houses seemed to be conspiring to get themselves made into a picture postcard. He went down the length of the Minster, past the Deanery, under the gothic arch of the Peterport and then, turning through almost a hundred and eighty degrees, down the steep cobbles of Chandlers Way.

To his right there were gracious eighteenth-century houses, monuments to successful merchants and sea captains of two hundred years ago. Between them he could see across the roofs of the town to the ocean. To his left after the Peterport there was the Deanery, then the battlemented garden wall, then the great grey slab side of the Minster itself, a lowering cliff pierced by windows. Then, a little further down the steep slope, opposite the merchant's house which was now where the Archdeacon lived, came the Cottages. Tiny they were, but beautiful; astonishing, yet inevitable, like a three-storey stage-set built in the very beginning against the great north wall of the Minster. Plaster and herring-bone brickwork and timber, somehow they fitted, although their seventeenth-century homeliness was three hundred years out of keeping with the great building against which they backed. Number 3, the Cottages. This was where Ted Barnes lived.

Septimus let his gaze travel up the narrow frontage to the twisted chimney smoking defiance at the gargoyle on the corner of the north aisle. He grinned. The chimney was festooned with more, and more complex, aerials than you would expect to find on the top of a television studio. Ted Barnes was a short-wave radio fanatic – a 'ham', and periodically he was in trouble with the Dean and Chapter because of the unsightliness of the uncouth aerials that sprouted like weeds from his roof. Ted always won the arguments because the Dean and Chapter always came to the same conclusion – they would never find as good an assistant verger for the same derisory wage.

Septimus hammered at the oak planks of the front door. There was a long pause and he was just making up his mind that Ted was out, when the door opened. It was Ted himself, a little man with a brown face, who looked more like a gamekeeper than a verger. He had a wide, mobile grin mostly dependent on a big mouth that could suddenly turn down at the corners and collapse into irredeemable tragedy.

'Mr Treloar,' said Ted, the corners of his mouth turning up like the sides of a bucket, 'come in, sir. I've got the kettle on the boil and Tokyo on the short wave.'

They went through the little parlour to the kitchen behind. There Ted made tea and then led the way into what had once been a scullery or back kitchen nestling under the very foundations of the cathedral like a mousehole under a palace. It was tiny, with one small window looking out on to Harry Tulloch's back door. It was here that Ted kept his 'ham' equipment, and indeed the microscopic room was as full of radio machinery as any broadcasting studio.

Septimus sat on a box, drank tea and listened to the vague echo of a squawking voice coming from the headphones over Ted's ears which – Ted assured him – was the voice of a real live veterinary surgeon living in a Tokyo suburb.

Ted pushed the headphones back from his ears and turned to Septimus.

'You know, sir,' he said, 'my vet, he's called Fuji-yama, near as I can make it. And Fuji-yama, he's got a daughter that's married to a man that was a baby in Hiroshima when the bomb was dropped. What do you think of that?'

Ted was knowledgeable about Tokyo. He knew a great deal about the problems of a Japanese vet, and he showed a definite inclination to want to talk about life in Tokyo. He was acrimonious and amusing about his battles with the Dean and Chapter over the aerials on the roof, but he added precisely nothing to what Harry Tulloch had said about the Minster ghost.

He saw Septimus to the door when Fuji-yama had signed off.

'Sorry I can't tell you more, Mr Treloar,' he said. 'Harry dug me out so I heard the organ playing when it shouldn't. And I've seen the light – just like Harry. If it was a light. We talked about it afterwards, but neither of us were sure.' He leaned forward, tapping Septimus confidentially on the shoulder. 'Mr Treloar, you want to have a word with the Archdeacon. He's a wise one is the Venerable Jenkins, and he don't believe in ghosts. Maybe he's got a theory. I'm mortal sure I haven't.'

Septimus went down Chandlers Way, past the great doors at the bottom of the Petersteps – closed for the night now, and so through the market where the stalls were putting up their shutters. He found the bookshop at the head of a steep alley leading down to the sea. It was a crumbling eighteenth-century house which had seen far better days. 'Sophia Wen-lock' was painted in peeling gold and gothic letters above the bow window. Septimus pulled the bell handle, setting off an old-fashioned clanking somewhere inside. He waited, gazing at the books in the window. A dog-eared edition of Dryden in twelve volumes. Scott's *Witchcraft* in folio, but in a modern binding. Boccaccio's *Decameron*, carefully opened at a nearly pornographic illustration. Foxed prints of the Minster. A mezzotint of the Petertower by moonlight. Septimus tried the bell again, but there was no answer, so he gave up and made his way back through the market to the car park at the bottom of Chandlers Way where he had left Grace looking after the landrover.

As he was about to turn into the car park he saw a cleric coming down Chandlers Way, a cleric glorious in gaiters and ecclesiastical frock coat.

'Good evening, Archdeacon,' said Septimus, mentally touching his forelock.

The Archdeacon paused very obviously, like an East Indiaman backing her mainsails. He looked at Septimus, gathering his wits.

'Ah Treloar, isn't it? Good evening. You've been doing your duty as guide to the visitors?' He made it sound as if the guide was marginally more deplorable than the visitors.

Septimus agreed.

'And I've been doing a bit of minor detecting,' he said. 'Archdeacon, Harry Tulloch tells me that you have ideas about these things that have been happening in the Minster. Lights. And the organ playing when it shouldn't.'

The Archdeacon hauled his watch from his waistcoat pocket and glared at it with manifest displeasure.

'I'm due at Sir John Stanhope's in ten minutes,' he said. 'I would not wish to be late. Sir John and I, we always dine together on a Monday, Treloar. Then after dinner we have a game of chess.'

'You're very welcome,' Septimus thought, although he did not put the thought into words ... Sir John Stanhope was next in line for the Lord Lieutenancy of the county. He was also the wealthiest fishmonger in the town.

'I mustn't keep you, sir,' said Septimus with devastating

23

humility. He looked very innocent and very baggy, the perfect epitome of a country parson. 'But I gathered you had ideas about what has been going on, and I should be honoured to hear your views.'

'Humbug!' said the Archdeacon, trying to impale Septimus on the stare that he usually reserved for meetings of assistant clergy. He was vaguely baffled when the innocent blue eyes simply refused to be impaled since they were always looking in the wrong direction.

'Humbug,' he said again. 'Someone playing feeble practical jokes. As you no doubt have been told, Treloar, I have spent the last twenty years investigating every conceivable sort of psychic phenomena.

'Ninety-five per cent is fraud. Four per cent is inexplicable. One per cent, perhaps, is genuine communication from the spirit world.' He pulled out his pocket watch again and studied it as if it were a psychic communication. 'I do not think that mysterious organ music and lights in the clerestory are likely to be part of that one per cent.' He put his watch back and looked severely at Septimus, as if it were all his fault. 'We are in the presence of a hoax, Treloar. And you of all people – an ex-police constable – ought to be aware of it. Meantime I must get to Sir John's'.

Septimus watched the upright figure stride away between the empty market stalls, and then went to the landrover.

'Grace,' he murmured as the dog licked his hand, 'if I were a psychic communication, I should grow spirit teeth and bite the venerable Aloysius in the calf.' But one thing he had noticed. The Archdeacon did believe in ghosts. That would be something to bear in mind.

'Course it's not haunted,' said Ted Barnes angrily, and slapped his pint tankard on to the table. 'Stands to reason. The Minster's been there for the better part of a thousand years. 'Taint been haunted before. Why should it be haunted now?'

Sophia Wenlock looked at him over the rim of her glass of gin and smiled a secret smile. She was a vastly fat woman, so that the smile made her eyes behind her spectacles disappear entirely.

'Ted Barnes,' she said, 'you and me, we know what we know. Ask the Archdeacon, Mr Barnes. He knows about spirits, don't he?'

Ted's face went red with anger and he snorted, so that Harry Tulloch put a restraining hand on his friend's arm.

'Watch it, Ted,' he said pacifically. 'Ain't no cause to get into a thratch. Nigh on closing time, anyway.' He turned to the woman. 'Time we was on our way, Mrs Wenlock.'

The two men came out of the Master Mariner as the Minster clock was striking ten. It was almost night and the moon was rising in the deep blue vault over the North Sea. The lights of the boats in the harbour twinkled like fairy lights.

'That woman,' said Ted, 'she riles me. Hang on a bit, Harry, while I get my cool back.' They went and leaned on the rail overlooking the harbour. Harry Tulloch produced cigarettes and they smoked and chatted, enjoying the gentleness of the night.

'What did she mean?' said Harry. 'Old Ma Wenlock, when she said that Himmler knows about spirits?' Harry usually called the Archdeacon Himmler.

'You know as well as I do. He's crackers on ghosts.'

'Ah. But it was the way she said it. She meant something more than that.'

Ted took a long pull at his cigarette so that the tip suddenly glowed bright in the darkness.

'She was a medium once, was old Ma Wenlock,' he said, 'before she took the bookshop. He went to one of her séances. Caught her twisting. Bits of wire for table lifting stuck up her knickers, or somesuch.'

'Did Himmler search her knickers?' asked Harry, genuinely interested.

'I don't know,' said Ted. 'But she gave up mediuming.'

Harry pondered this, gazing out at the dark sea.

'Be like looking for a hair grip in a bell tent,' he said. 'Pair of bell tents. Pink nylon.'

There were footsteps coming along the pavement behind them, brisk and purposeful.

Ted turned to see who it was.

'Talk of the devil,' he said. 'Here he is himself.'

'Been playing chess with Jackie Stanhope,' said Harry. 'Always does on a Monday, regular as a clock . . . Evening, sir.'

The Archdeacon acknowledged the greeting and sailed on up the steep slope of Chandlers Way. The cobbles were beginning to gleam under the moon, and his shadow was black across them.

'Ah, well,' said Harry, 'I'm for my bed.'

Ted glanced up at the Minster clock. 'Quarter of an hour and I've got a date with a film cameraman in San Francisco. It's morning there, Harry. Bet they don't have no haunted Minsters in San Francisco.'

'Only on the films,' said Harry.

They set off up the hill after the Archdeacon.

'Hark!' said Harry suddenly, stopping in his tracks. There was the sound of music over their heads. Organ music, soft at first but growing louder. A joyous cataract of sound as if someone was putting his whole soul into his flying fingers. The Archdeacon had stopped in front of them. They could see his face, white in the moonlight, as he gazed up at the great blank windows along the north side of the Minster.

Without comment the two vergers ran until they came

up with the Archdeacon. He held up his hand – listening. The music swelled behind the dark windows of the nave.

'Look!' said Ted, panting from the run up the steep hill. He pointed to the window over the roof of the Petersteps. There was a light, a wavering lantern. They could see the greens and blues of the stained glass, the sudden diamond gleam of a clear pane. The light moved slowly eastward, wavered and vanished, only to appear a moment later at the next window.

'Come!' said the Archdeacon. 'I have my keys.' He led the way at a stumbling run up the hill, through the Peterport, past the Deanery and back along the south side of the Minster. Ted Barnes, because he was the youngest, quickly took the lead. He reached the door that led through the cloister and into the cathedral on the south side, and there he had to wait, leaning back on the stonework, panting. He had left his own keys in his cassock pocket.

The Archdeacon came up and after a moment's fumbling, threw open the door. They hurried down the dark cloister, the organ still playing – in front of them now. Once again the Archdeacon grappled with keys and flung the door open. With a twinge of astonishment as he stepped into the nave the Archdeacon realized that for the first time in his life he was afraid. The great church was dappled with moonlight and shadow – black and blue, white and silver, and soft pastel shades where the moon shone through coloured glass. The light had vanished from the clerestory, but the cavern of the nave was filled with the sound of the organ. There was something strange about it. It was quite loud, but remote: echoing like an organ played in some vast sea cave, with the music going back and back from sunless cavern to sunless cavern, and the sea rolling and thundering beneath. There was something else different, something to do with the range of the instrument itself, but the Archdeacon could not identify what it was.

'Come on!' he said and led the way toward the organ. As they reached the centre aisle he said, 'Tulloch, you go to the top of the Petersteps. Watch the bottom of the circular stairs in case anyone tries to come down that way.'

Obediently Harry blundered off in the darkness.

It was black under the organ, and the Archdeacon groped, trying to find the switch for the light on the stairs up to the organ loft. As he groped, the organ music faded. There was a crackling silence, and then from over their heads came a terrible scream which echoed through the building and faded away into nothing. At that moment the Archdeacon's groping hand came into contact with the switch. He turned on the light over the wooden stairs, and to the eternal credit of his courage, ran up them, leaving Ted Barnes at the bottom.

There was nothing to see in the organ loft. Just a locked keyboard and a litter of music and battered hymn books. Neither was there anything along the clerestory walkway. Nor down the circular stairs leading from the clerestory to the Petersteps. The door at the bottom was locked, and Harry Tulloch was standing outside it.

In silence the three men walked back toward the south door, more shaken than they would have cared to admit.

A shadow stirred in the darkness of the cloister, and a high, thin voice spoke.

'Good evening.' The Archdeacon started as if someone had suddenly fired a pistol.

'Sorry if I startled you, but I was on my way home and I heard the organ.'

It was Mr Berwick the organist, urbane, unflappable as always.

'Yes,' said the Archdeacon, 'an intruder. Unfortunately

we failed to catch him. He was playing your organ, I fear.'

'*My* organ?' said Berwick. They were walking down the cloister and he paused to strike a match on the wall. His thin, sardonic face was brightly illuminated as he lit a cigarette. '*My* organ? I fear it's a bit more complicated than that, my dear Archdeacon. You see . . . the foot pedals were all wrong. You couldn't play like that – not on my organ. You can make what you like of it, venerable sir, but I rather fancy you have been treated to what the instrument sounded like – oh! any time between 1750 and 1935. That was when my organ was put in.'

He dropped the match and there was darkness in the cloister.

3   Consulting Detective

The Reverend Septimus Treloar marshalled his thoughts as he drove the landrover along the straight road beside the Danedyke on his way to Minster Saint Peter. In the middle of breakfast the phone had rung. It had been the Dean, with a concise account of what had happened on the previous evening.

'M-my dear Septimus,' he had said, 'I would be m-most obliged if you would come and investigate us.' The Dean stammered only when he was perturbed, and Septimus could understand his anxiety. Whatever was going on must soon result in undesirable publicity. Septimus smiled, remembering the conversation.

'Headlines in the *Daily M-mirror*. And G-god save us all, the Archdeacon is threatening to investigate.' He changed gear and dropped speed as he came to the outskirts of the town.

What facts were there? Precious few so far. Alisdair Cameron had heard the organ and a scream, and had seen someone carrying a light. That had been at one o'clock in the morning over a month ago. Then last night – at about ten-thirty, Harry Tulloch, Ted Barnes, the Archdeacon and Berwick had seen and heard the same. An odd difference in time, and ten-thirty was early for any ghost – fake or real. And Berwick said the organ sounded as it must have done half a century ago.

Septimus stopped for a pedestrian crossing and scowled at

a woman with a pram. It was all such nonsense. If you ruled out the supernatural, it appeared to be totally without point. And niggling and nagging at his mind was the question of how it was done. A light had to be carried by somebody. Well, presumably there had been plenty of time before the Archdeacon and the vergers had got round to the south door. The Minster abounded in hiding places. But that only brought him back to the question 'why?'

Then there was the music. Was it played on the organ? Not if it had stopped when the Archdeacon said it did. Anyway, it couldn't be if Berwick was to be believed. And that meant a record player or a tape recorder. But what sort of electronic instrument would produce the volume of sound involved? And where was it? And who operated it? And why? ... He cursed, tramping on the brakes as he turned into the car park, nearly hitting a motor cyclist coming out. The motor cyclist snarled at him. 'Sorry!' he shouted, knowing he was to blame.

The motor cyclist was young and his face was vaguely familiar, but Septimus hardly noticed as he grappled with the question 'why?'

The car park was at the bottom of Chandlers Way. He left the landrover and walked across the market to the Peter-steps. As he mounted them he admired as he always did the delicate fan vaulting high over his head. At the top of the steps, just before the nave door there was a roped-off area with men inside it taking up the flagstones. Septimus remembered that there was work going on for a new heating system.

The great building was thronged with holidaymakers, loud with the sound of echoing feet and children's voices. Septimus went and sat in the centre of the nave looking eastward toward the Victorian screen, the organ behind it to the left, beyond that the high altar, and then as a great coloured back-drop the east window in the far distance. On either side of the nave, like two ranks of giant men-at-arms, marched the great Norman pillars, holding up the roof as they had done for the better part of a thousand years. At the top of each pillar, just below the capital, hung a long, grey, metal loudspeaker, one unit in the Minster's public address system. Well, that was one way you could do it. Connect a tape to the public address system. At least you'd get enough volume that way. Fill the Minster with sound.

Ted Barnes, sober in a cassock, was coming down the aisle. Septimus suddenly remembered the motor cyclist in the car park. 'Hullo, Ted,' he said, 'I've just seen your lad. I was so busy thinking about this mullarkey with the organ that I nearly ran over him.'

Ted looked startled for a moment and then grinned. 'Ah. Home for a long week-end, Norman. Just gone off back to Cambridge. Works for the Post Office now, does Norman. You didn't run over him – not serious like – I take it?'

Septimus shook his head. 'Missed him by inches. So busy thinking about this organ business that I didn't even recognize him.'

Ted sat down in the pew. 'It's a right queer business, Mr Treloar, and that's a fact. What d'you make of it, sir?'

Septimus pointed up at the speaker of the nearest pillar 'Where d'you control those from, Ted?'

Looking at the verger's brown, humorous face, Septimus could see the idea slowly taking shape in his mind.

Ted grinned. 'Well now, that's a thought,' he said. 'You could do it that way. Give you enough volume and all.' He stood up. 'I'll show you.' He led the way down the nave.

Beneath the organ, screened from the body of the church, there was a big switchboard in an oak cupboard. It was screwed to the back of the organ casing. Ted opened the doors and pointed inside.

'This is the master switch. Each one of them knobs controls a speaker, one for each pillar. And them's the mikes. Pulpit. Altar. Choir pulpit. Dean. Precentor ... and old uncle Tom Cobley and all.'

Septimus looked at the banks of switches. 'Could you put a tape recorder into that lot?' he asked.

'Easy,' said Ted, pointing. 'That's the amplifier. If you fed it in at the back of that ... you'd get it out of all the speakers.' He scratched his head, grinning. 'Organ music. Vintage pre-1935. Fill the church it would.'

Septimus tapped the oak boarding to which the control panel was fixed.

'What's inside here?'

'Works of the organ,' said Ted. 'Want to have a look?'

He took keys from his pocket and unlocked a door which was simply a panel in the casing. 'There's a light, somewhere,' he said, groping. There was a click and then in a perspective of light and shadow Septimus could see a complication of pipes and tubes. There were wires everywhere.

'Didn't realize an organ had so many bits,' said Septimus.

'This isn't the half of it,' said Ted. 'There's this much again underneath in the crypt.'

The boarding at the back of the control panel for the public address system was festooned with a maze of grey cables which led down through the floor.

They came out from the claustrophobic little room and Ted locked the door.

'The Archdeacon, he's talking about a full scale investigation,' he said.

'He don't believe in ghosts, the Archdeacon. Me, I think it's a fiddle. But I'm damned if I know how it's done. D'you, Mr Treloar?'

'Search me,' said Septimus.

He wandered out of the Minster into the bright sunlight of Cloister Garth. He strolled across the grass to the fountain in the middle and sat on the stone edge, looking at the fish.

Alisdair Cameron came out of the Deanery front door, saw him sitting there, and came across the grass.

'I heard my dad phone you this morning,' he said. 'Consulting detective.'

Septimus nodded. 'That's it, Alisdair.'

'Do you remember what Sherlock said? When you've eliminated everything that is impossible, what remains must be the truth.' He was standing with his hands on the stone, gazing into the pool. Suddenly he looked up, almost fiercely, flicking the hair out of his eyes. 'Do you think it's supernatural, Septimus?'

Septimus took out his pipe and clamped it between his teeth.

'Alisdair,' he said, 'I spent most of my life as a copper. I never investigated anything that hadn't got some sort of a villain at the back of it. Nearest I got to spirits was a fake medium who thieved a diamond brooch.'

Alisdair made a sudden grab into the water, trying to catch one of the carp. 'But why?' he said. 'What on earth's the point?'

'That,' said Septimus between puffs as he lit his pipe, 'is the sixty-four thousand dollar question. Now come on Alisdair, my lad. I've got a date with your father.'

Septimus and the Dean sat in the great eighteenth-century bow window of the study. It looked out over the Archdeacon's garden on the far side of Chandlers Way, over the harbour and out to sea. To the left there was a foreshortened view of the Cottages, the north wall of the Minster hanging above them like a cliff.

The Dean was worried. The Minster was his responsibility.

'It's the notoriety m-my dear Septimus. We shall have the M-minster full of ghost hunters. And one on the Chapter is m-more than enough.'

'The Archdeacon doesn't believe in ghosts,' said Septimus.

The Dean cocked a shrewd eye at him.

'No? But if you spend all your life trying to prove a negative . . . perhaps you fear there m-might be a positive at the heart of it after all. King Saul banned necromancy, Septimus. M-made it a capital offence. But he still consulted the Witch of Endor.' Septimus said nothing. It was a perceptive point.

They discussed the problem for half an hour without clarifying it, though the conversation helped Septimus to build up a picture of the staff of the Minster, of those who would know its geography, of those who would hold keys. The trouble was there were too many of them. All the residentiary canons, the vergers, the electrician, the part-time librarian, even the women who did the flowers. Septimus had a sudden delirious vision of thousands upon thousands of Minster keys, all as big as the keys of Saint Peter, in handbags and pockets, on tables and hooks, all over East Anglia. The place was about as secure as Euston station in the rush hour.

'Have you formed any theories, Septimus?'

He looked sourly at the Dean. Amateurs always talked about theories, whereas real detection was more like bricklaying.

'No,' he said, 'not yet. I've got a few ideas. Pretty vague. I'll keep them to myself if you don't mind.'

The Dean grinned impishly and suddenly looked like his son.

'Meaning I'm number one on your suspect list? Very right and proper, Chief Inspector.'

In his turn Septimus smiled. He had not expected the Dean to be quite-that quick on the uptake. But he answered easily.

'Yes. You're number one and underlined in red. If you don't know "how?" or "why?", "who?" might be anybody, and the only person I know didn't do it is me.'

'Excellent,' said the Dean. 'So I take it I may not know your plans?'

'No,' said Septimus, 'but who would you put bottom of your list of suspects?'

The Dean answered without hesitation. 'Harry Tulloch. He's been part of the Minster all his life. Never been any-where else – apart from the War. His father was head verger, and Harry was a choirboy. Then he was verger him-self. He's been head verger since 1950. I should be not a little surprised if the culprit turned out to be Harry Tulloch.'

Septimus found Harry Tulloch at the top of the Petersteps. He was leaning over the barrier talking to a workman who was well down into the earth beneath the flagstones. The dry brown soil looked odd, heaped on the grey stone. It was as if a piece of garden had run into the Minster for sanctuary.

'Harry, I want to talk to you,' said Septimus.

'Coming, Major,' said the verger. He gave a final admon-ition to the foreman. 'So whatever you do, Sam, you've got to keep half the passage clear. Can't have the visitors falling into your hole. His Nibs wouldn't like it. Now then, Major, I'm at your disposal, as the actress said to the bishop.'

'Private,' said Septimus.

They went together to Harry's cubby-hole and Harry closed the door.

'Harry, the Dean's asked me to investigate this business of the organ.'

'Damn good job, too,' said Harry. 'His Nibs shows a glimmering of sense every now and then.'

'Harry, I don't want anyone but you to know this. Even the Dean doesn't know it. I'm going to take up residence in the Minster.'

'You're going to sleep here?' Harry looked astonished for a moment. Then he recovered. 'Good idea, Major. Think I'll join you. Be quite like old times.'

'No, not yet, Harry. Maybe need you later.'

'Where are you going to sleep, sir?'

'Under the organ – where the works are. Now look, Harry . . . if anything happens, if you hear the organ, or see any lights, or if you get knocked up because someone else has, don't come round and through the south door. Whatever anyone says, you belt down Chandlers Way and cover the bottom of the Petersteps. Is that clear?'

Harry thought about this. 'Yes,' he said, 'I see. You can leave out the west door because we haven't opened that since they churched Queen Victoria's grandmother. So it only leaves the south door and the Petersteps. Unless he gets in through the drains. I'll do that, Major.'

There was a knock on the door and Ted Barnes stuck his head round.

'Harry, you'd better come,' he said. 'Those blokes digging that hole for the new pipes. They've found a coffin.'

4　An Organist Called Primrose

They had, too. Septimus and Harry stood by the barrier and looked down into the four-foot hole in the dry earth. At the bottom they could see the tapering sides of a coffin lid, the oak appearing surprisingly new for all the years it had been buried. Sam the foreman was in the hole, carefully digging away the loose earth, working upward toward the head of the coffin. A crowd of tourists was beginning to gather, peering and craning, blocking the top of the Peter-steps.

'I'll have to stop this,' said Harry. 'Right old traffic jam.'

'There's letters,' said the foreman. He crouched down, clearing the incised carving with his finger nails. Because he was working from the foot of the coffin upward, the inscription came back to front into the light.

1737 - 1772
Hezekiah Primrose
R.I.P.

'And who was Hezekiah Primrose?' asked Septimus.

'One of my revered predecessors,' said a voice in his ear. Septimus spun round. The answer had come so pat as to be startling. It was Berwick, the organist, and he was smiling remotely, as if at some secret joke of his own.

'Hezekiah Primrose was Master of the Music from 1761 until he was murdered in 1772.'

'Now come along, ladies and gentlemen,' said Harry loudly. 'Move along, please. You're causing an obstruction.' He dropped his voice and spoke to the foreman. 'Sam you'll have to leave that hole. Can't dig up an organist. Better get some sacks over the coffin. Ted . . .' He searched the holiday crowd, looking for his assistant. 'Ted. You lock the door at the bottom of the Petersteps. Put a notice on it. "Temporarily Out of Use." Tell 'em they'll have to use the south door . . . Now come along, ladies and gentlemen. Move along, please.' He shooed the holidaymakers into the nave and turned to Septimus. 'Excuse me, Major. I'll have to go and tell His Nibs about this.'

The crowd began to disperse unwillingly. Septimus stood a moment, looking into the hole, and then wandered into the Minster himself.

'So far as I know, Primrose was the only Master of Music who distinguished himself by getting murdered.' Berwick was tall, stoop-shouldered so that he looked a little like a vulture. His yellow face was full of sardonic glee. 'Come, Mr Treloar. I'll show you something.'

With Ted Barnes at his elbow Septimus followed the organist. He led them to the wall just beside the door and pointed to a marble tablet. Septimus judged it must be almost exactly in line with the grave at the top of the Petersteps. The inscription was very short.

'Is your Latin up to translating it?' asked Berwick.

'No,' said Septimus.

'Nor's mine,' said Ted.

'Hezekiah Primrose,' said Berwick. 'Born July 10 1737. Master of Music 1761 to 1772. The thread of his life was violently cut off on the 14th of August.'

'Violently cut off?' said Septimus.

'Yes,' Berwick replied. 'With a knife, as a matter of fact. A seaman's knife. You can read all the lurid details in the Chapter library. It's all in old Lovebody's Journal.'

'I'll do that,' said Septimus. He had heard of Lovebody. He had been a residentiary canon for a large part of the eighteenth century, and for nearly fifty years he had kept a voluminous diary. The more interesting and least improper parts of it had been published.

'You'll find it most illuminating,' said Berwick. 'If you care to come to the Chapter library, I will be delighted to act as Virgil to your Dante.'

'Hang on for me, Mr Berwick,' said Ted. 'I've just got to lock the door and do that notice for Harry. Five minutes, then I'll be with you. Proper fascinating, this is.'

The Chapter library was a dark room on the south side of the Minster, close to Harry's cubby-hole. It had once been a chantry chapel.

When Ted Barnes joined them Berwick had already found the published edition of Lovebody's Journal, and was sitting at the long table in the centre of the room turning over the pages. Septimus waited patiently, watching the sun as it struggled through the dark glass of a Victorian window, full of stiff figures of former bishops. The window was dirty. The room smelt of dust and old leather.

Berwick looked up as Ted came in.

'Here we are,' he said. He turned another page and started to read. '1772. August 15th. This day a sensation as I foresaw. All the Chapter in a taking. Canon Price prating of the horsemen of the Apocalypse, and the Dean sent for post from London. He hath not been here these six months. Mayhap he hath forgotten that the Minster is part of his duties. It fell out as I foreshowed to Primrose – him but a child in the cruel ways of the little blind god . . .' Berwick stopped reading and looked up. 'He means Cupid,' he said. '. . . But he would not take warning from a head wiser than his own. Now the silver cord is loosed and he "hath gone to his long home" as Holy Writ says. Or rather, he is violently slain. A very Uriah dying for his Bathsheba. Indeed, not in the forefront of the battle as the Book of Kings tells us, but where – as I suppose – he would be. On his own organ stool . . .'

'Wicked old man,' thought Septimus. 'He positively enjoyed it.'

Berwick's high, dry voice went on.

'Thus it fell out. Janet, his doxy, being with child, and her a married woman, Primrose took – I fancy – the hint I gave him. I could no less, he being my pupil, my child of the flesh.

'Her husband is a seaman. Captain of the brig *Pelican*. Seen off the headland on Tuesday and expected in harbour last night. Captain John Jancey. Him not ashore these ten months, and her three months with child! I name no names but the sea light in the Minster Tower failed last night, as I saw returning from my carousal. And the organ playing. Yet – despite the lack of the light – the brig *Pelican* avoided the rocks and, which are worse, the banks of sand, and against all hope came safe to harbour. I say no more, for all is speculation. But Primrose was found dead with the dawn, his life's blood on the keys of the organ. They say it was a seaman's knife in his back.'

A bluebottle droned sleepily round the inkwell in front of Berwick, otherwise there was a long silence in the library. It was broken by the opening of the door. The Archdeacon came in.

'Ah, Barnes,' he said. 'What's this I hear? About a coffin?'

'That's right, sir,' said Ted. 'Top of the Petersteps. The heating men dug it up.'

'I greatly hope they have *not* dug it up. Most unseemly.'

'Only in a manner of speaking, sir. They uncovered it like.'

'One of my predecessors,' said Berwick. 'The ill-starred Hezekiah Primrose. We have just been looking him up in Lovebody's Journal.'

'Wicked old man,' said Septimus.

'Mr Treloar,' the Archdeacon said severely, 'I thought your duty ended yesterday. I do not doubt that your parish would be glad to see you.'

'Yes,' said Septimus, equable and ambiguous, 'but I was interested in the discovery of the coffin.'

The Archdeacon looked at his watch. 'No doubt you have work to do, Mr Barnes.'

'Oh,' said Ted, startled, 'yes.' He went out of the door.

'And I've got a lunch date,' said Berwick. 'If vergers take a hint, can Masters of Music be far behind? Good day Archdeacon, Mr Treloar.'

'No,' said Septimus, flopping into the chair vacated by Berwick and flipping over the pages of the Journal. 'No. I've neither work nor date. Country parsons only work on Sundays. Anyway, I'm having a day off.'

The Archdeacon cleared his throat loudly. 'I see,' he said.

There was silence in the library, so that Septimus was suddenly aware of the bluebottle.

'An angry, angular man,' thought Septimus. 'I wonder why? And I wonder why he wants to get rid of me?'

The Archdeacon put his hands behind his back and walked slowly across the library. Septimus watched him without appearing to do so. The Archdeacon stopped suddenly.

'Treloar,' he said without turning, 'Treloar, has the Dean asked you to investigate this – ah – haunting?'

'No,' said Septimus with immediate and engaging dishonesty.

The Archdeacon turned and came pacing back across the

42

library. He was pontifical, ponderous, his hands still clasped behind his back.

'Good,' he said, 'excellent! I hoped Charles would have the wisdom to desist. It really is not a matter for policemen . . .' He paused, gazing at his toes, as if he was considering some affair of great gravity.

'Treloar. I gather you had some little reputation before you were ordained. But I take it you have never investigated an – ah – haunting in the course of your policeman's duties?'

'No,' said Septimus, grinning to himself inside the stone mask of his serious and innocent face. 'No, sir. I can't say I've any experience of ghosts.' There was of course the fake medium and the diamond brooch. But he did not feel inclined to tell the Archdeacon about that.

'Well, how could you?' said the Archdeacon magnanimously. 'Twenty years with sneak-thieves and traffic offenders. And now a country parish.'

'As you say,' murmured Septimus, his face like a stone po.

'But of course I have,' continued the Archdeacon, starting to pace up and down again.

Just like Jancey on the quarterdeck of the *Pelican* thought Septimus, inconsequentially. 'Flog 'em at the gratings!'

'I should be most interested to hear your views, sir,' he murmured with the humility of a performing bear hoping for a bun.

'Umm.' The Archdeacon grunted, still pacing. 'In my time I have investigated many psychic phenomena. I have exposed not a few frauds. And I have very little doubt that this is another . . .' He stopped in his tracks and looked full at Septimus.

'And yet, Treloar . . .'

Septimus frankly studied the harsh lines of the Archdeacon's humourless face. The eyes were full of what Septimus could only describe as 'longing'. The Archdeacon suddenly looked away and started to pace the library again. Septimus waited, self-contained, certain that something else would come. The bluebottle was buzzing angrily at the feet of a nineteenth-century bishop. The sound of tourists came faintly through the closed door. The Archdeacon had his back to Septimus. He was standing at one of the glass-fronted bookcases, apparently examining its contents.

'Treloar. I am a lonely man. I have no close relatives. I have devoted all my life to psychic research. To the cause of truth. To exposing fraud where I could find it . . .'

'Yes,' said Septimus gently, 'the search for truth. There must be truth somewhere.'

'Indeed,' said the Archdeacon with sudden violence. He stretched up and took a leather-bound book from above his head. 'Berwick read you a passage from Lovebody's Journal. But Berwick knows nothing. He has not read this – the original. I have. I edited the Minster History, you know.'

He sat down, turning the crackling pages of the book so that Septimus could see the crabbed handwriting, the faded ink.

'Very little of this has ever been published. Much of it is unpublishable.' He looked severely at Septimus over the top of the book. 'Lovebody was a whoremonger. A licentious old man who was a disgrace to his cloth.' He tapped the book with his forefinger. 'What followed from the death of Primrose is mixed with the most disgusting details of his liaison with a girl called Rachel. I shall read you what is relevant, omitting the remainder.

'Now listen to this – nearly a year after Primrose's murder. 1773. August 9th. Last night I heard him. It gone midnight and Rachel coming to the servants' entrance. I, opening the door, heard the organ . . .

'August 10th. Last night again the organ. I am afraid. The dreadful anniversary approaches, and it was I who advised Primrose, and him but a young man unschooled in the ways of vice. There is a God above all, could I but turn to Him . . .

'August 12th. In the dark of the night to the very door of the Minster. I am drawn as a moth to the candle. May the Lord Jesus have mercy on my poor soul. The night dark and him playing. There were footsteps, and I did think I saw his lantern. I am very afraid. Whither shall I turn? Only Rachel comforts me now . . .

'August 13th. Tonight the sea light extinguished. The night is wrong, for it should have been tomorrow. They should not have buried him where they did, for that is the way the other comes, and I am persuaded it draws him. The dead over the grave of the dead. And to what assignation? Mercy. Mercy. Mercy.

'August 15th. It is ended. Last night I saw him and he looked at me, and him in his grave these ten months.

'I was drawn by the playing. So gay the music, but my heart cold with terror. I stood within the doorway. God help me, I could no other, and the music a dance of the damned. He came. I saw him on the walkway. He is bigger than I thought, for I never saw him in life, and he is bearded and in his sea clothes. And he looked on me, his face livid from the rope. And he knew my part in it. So they played out their devil's play. Primrose screamed as he died. I had not thought of that, and there is but one end for me who am guilty as hell itself . . .' The Archdeacon closed the Journal with a little thump. 'Well, Treloar?'

Septimus stirred. What was the Archdeacon at? Was he trying to prove something? And if so, to whom? Himself – or Septimus?

'Remorse,' he said. 'Drink, and a guilty conscience. Evidently he led Primrose off the straight and narrow. Even seems to have suggested that he try to kill Jancey. The anniversary of the death preyed on his mind – and I'm not surprised.'

'It could be,' said the Archdeacon. 'He died a fortnight later screaming about Captain Jancey.' He got up and returned the Journal to its shelf. He locked the glass front of the case and put the key back in a drawer.

'Someone trying to reconstruct the story?' said Septimus.

'Possibly,' said the Archdeacon. For once he was not pompous – just grave. 'Possibly. But it is strange that they should have discovered Primrose's grave today. Nobody could have known that would happen.'

'The ghost got his dates wrong,' said Septimus irreverently. 'Last night was the 9th. It should have been the 8th according to Lovebody.'

5   Doings in the Night

Septimus stood alone in the centre aisle of the Minster and watched the sun go down behind the west window. At the top of the window were the greens and blues of heaven, with serried ranks of martyrs, prophets and saints. In the centre, seated on a throne, there was a stern Christ, holding the balances of judgement. At the bottom there were murky reds and flaming crimsons, horrific medieval devils and the twisted shapes of the damned. It was quiet in the Minster, peaceful after the thronging visitors of the day. But the window did not speak of peace, only of judgement.

Septimus thought of the tortured soul of Canon Lovebody, and wondered what had really happened to that eighteenth-century clerical roué.

He stood gazing at the window while the light died and the shadows lengthened. What had happened on that night nearly two hundred years ago?

Evidently Primrose had fallen in love with Janet Jancey. She had become pregnant while her husband was at sea. So much was clear, but what followed was obscure. It looked as if Primrose had tried to wreck the big *Pelican* by extinguishing the light in the Petertower. The attempt had failed, and then . . .? Well, according to Lovebody, Jancey had murdered Primrose. If he had indeed been hung for the crime, there would probably be a record of the court proceedings somewhere. Anyway, what had it to do with twentieth-century practical jokes with the organ? For the moment he gave it up and strolled quietly down the aisle to his temporary bedroom under the organ. During the afternoon he had driven home, changed into slacks, plimsolls and an old rollneck sweater, and collected what he needed for the night. He made up his bed, rolling out his sleeping bag on a mattress of hassocks. He took a big torch and a pork pie from his pack and went on a round of the Minster, swinging the one and contentedly munching the other.

As he prowled round the building the light faded and the shadows deepened. He came to the Lady Chapel where the tiny wick of the lamp that burned before the Sacrament threw shadows like the silent surge of a distant sea. Impelled by some inner urge he knelt for a while, listening to quietness. Surprised, he found he was praying for the soul of old Lovebody, and the organist, and the sea captain who had murdered him. 'Mercy. Mercy. Mercy,' the wretched old man had written. In his years with the police Septimus had seen precious little mercy. He was now old enough to understand its importance. He could only hope that Lovebody had found it. Grinning wryly at the contradictions in his own character, he got up and continued his silent prowl. Harry Tulloch's cubby-hole was locked. So was the Dean's vestry, and the door leading down to the crypt, and the Chapter library. He went on down the aisle, tried the south door, crossed the nave by the shadowy font, and so came back along the north aisle to the top of the Petersteps. He went down the steps. The door at the bottom leading out into the market was secure. As he tried it he could hear a drunk singing in the market-place.

'My name is Macnamara, I'm the leader of the band . . .'

'Bit early to have that much of a skinful,' Septimus murmured as he went back up the steps. He shone his torch into the excavation where Hezekiah Primrose was buried. The sacks were in place over the coffin, but the door to the circular stairway on the far side of the excavation was ajar. Septimus frowned a moment, then his face cleared as he realized that the workmen were digging at the bottom of the stairs, so, for the moment, the door had to be open. He clambered round the open grave, stumbling over heaped earth and piled stone, and so on to the stairs. He went up, turning all the time, using his torch. He passed the door that led out on to the clerestory and went on up to the Lantern itself. It seemed a never-ending climb, but at last he arrived, not a little out of breath. He pushed open the door and gazed in at the unbearably bright light which was reflected back from an octagon of glass, black because of the night outside. Not wishing to be seen all over the town, he did not go in but he suddenly thought of Primrose coming up the circular stairs as he was said to have done. Presumably the Lantern was lit by oil in those days. In his imagination he could see the brig riding between the rocks and the treacherous sands outside the harbour. He could hear the creak of her rigging, the 'ting-tang' of the ship's bell, the sound of bare feet on planking. He could see in his mind Jancey – a big man with a beard – straining his eyes through a sea mist for the light that was not there. Septimus closed the little door and went back down the stone steps.

He came out on to the clerestory which seemed almost light after the dark stairs. East and west the walkway stretched into the shadows, great windows on one side, a wide balustrade guarding the drop into the nave on the other. Between window and window, where it passed through the vaulting springing from the tops of the massive pillars, the walkway dived into a little, gothic arched tunnel. The whole arrangement, Septimus decided, looked like nothing so much as a series of boxes in a theatre, a great window at the back of each box, and each box connected to the next by a narrow corridor of stone.

He turned left, eastward, towards the organ.

Half-way down the walkway he stopped. There had been a noise from somewhere on the far side of the nave. He crept forward out of one of the tunnels and peeped down, keeping his head low so as not to be silhouetted against the window behind him.

There was a light in the shadows on the far side of the nave. Someone with a torch was coming through the south door. He could see the torchlight in the glazed porch. The inner door opened and the torch stabbed down the south aisle, and Septimus heard the hiss of the hydraulic piston as the inner door closed. The torch moved westward down the aisle, its beam cut off by pillars, only to reappear a moment later. It stopped half-way down the nave and remained steady by a tomb at the base of a pillar. Evidently it had been put down on top of the tomb. He could see a dark figure moving in and out of the torchlight, stooping, doing something at the base of the tomb.

Bent nearly double, he ran silently along the clerestory to the wooden stairs that led down past the organ loft, and so out beneath the organ by the door to his temporary bedroom. A darker shadow among the shadows, he went back up the north side of the nave until he was opposite the torch. Then on hands and knees he crept between the pews. As he reached the centre aisle the intruder stood up and the torch gleamed momentarily on a white face and a white clerical collar. It was the Archdeacon.

Carrying his torch the Archdeacon came between the pews to the centre aisle. Septimus lay flat, wondering what he would do if the Archdeacon trod on him. Pretend to be blind drunk? Or say he was doing a brass rubbing? But the Archdeacon turned right down the aisle and his torch disappeared beneath the organ.

Septimus reversed his tracks down the pews and the north

aisle until, his big body behind a pillar, he could see under the organ. Once again the Archdeacon had rested his torch on a convenient ledge. This time he was doing something to the controls of the public address system. He worked for five minutes, then picked up his torch and went down the centre aisle. Septimus watched the torch flick into the porch of the south door, he heard the hiss of the hydraulic piston and the click as the outer door locked. He waited a full two minutes and then went to look at the public address system. Instinct born of long practice told him to touch nothing before he had made a thorough inspection. It was as well that instinct came to his aid. At the top, between frame and door, the Archdeacon had secured a thin piece of black cotton which must break if the door were opened. Septimus smiled. 'The Ven. Aloysius must have been rubbing up on his detective novels,' he murmured.

Down the aisle, at the foot of the tomb of an unknown crusader he found a big tape recorder. Surprisingly for its size, it appeared to be battery-operated. His fingers on the lid told Septimus that it was running. Well, whatever it was for, it was certain that it was not going to produce a noise that would sound like the organ.

He opened it and inspected the controls with his torch.

'Well! Well!' he said out loud. 'What a clever Archdeacon!' The recorder had been modified in several ways. It carried the largest spools possible and it was moving more slowly than Septimus had ever seen a tape-recorder move before. He guessed that it would be several hours before the machine ran out of tape.

Struck by a sudden thought, he altered the controls, ran the tape back, and then set the machine to replay. A few moments and he heard his own voice saying, 'Well! Well! What a clever Archdeacon!' He found the microphone between the feet of the unknown crusader. He set the controls back to record and then, standing by the feet of the crusader, he said in a sepulchral voice, 'I am the ghost of Septimus Treloar. The Venerable Aloysius Jenkins murdered me ...' He played this piece of nonsense back for his own amusement and then regretfully erased it by running the tape back to the beginning. He would dearly have loved to leave it for the Archdeacon, but he had to remember that he was involved in a serious investigation. He left the tape-recorder and went back to his hideout beneath the organ.

Before he slept Septimus gave some thought to the Archdeacon. At least he could be written off the notional suspect list since he appeared to be investigating himself. Or, on second thoughts ... could he? That sort of evidence could be used in more than one way. Septimus had plenty of experience of the art of alibi. His mind wandered back over their strange conversation in the Chapter library. 'There must be truth somewhere.' He fancied that the Archdeacon would like to prove one genuine, thirty-two carat ghost before he died ... So he drifted into sleep.

He awoke suddenly, completely, and had slid out of his sleeping bag before he identified the sound which had wakened him. Someone had tiptoed past the door of his hidey-hole. He looked at the illuminated dial of his watch. It was nearly two o'clock. He slipped into his pumps and cautiously slid the door open. There was nothing but darkness. the heavy torch in his hand, he stepped out, crept soundlessly into the choir and sat in one of the back stalls, his ears straining. There was nothing. The Minster was dark. In front of him the great windows to the south were hardly visible against the clouded sky. But then on the far side of the choir, coming down the aisle from the Lady Chapel he saw a light, a silver sword in the blackness, extinguished almost as suddenly as it stabbed out. Someone had switched on a torch to get his bearings.

He went across the choir to the deep shadows by the Bishop's throne. He waited, but saw nothing more. He crossed the aisle to the doorway of the Dean's vestry, then to Harry Tulloch's cubby-hole, and from there to the Chapter library. He leaned on the stonework, looking round the arch, his shoulder on the door itself. The door stirred and creaked and opened an inch. Suddenly Septimus was very still. The library had been locked earlier in the evening.

He pushed the door open with his foot. It creaked loudly in the darkness. He stood to one side of the arch for a full minute, waiting. But there was no sound of movement from inside. With great care, his back pressed against the stone, he slid into the library. Then he whipped the door closed, using his torch now, the bright beam like lightning in the dark room.

There was nothing. He shone the torch round. There were three cupboards. He tried the doors. They were all locked and there was no other hiding place. There was nothing to show that anyone had been into the library except the unlocked door and . . . Septimus paused. The beam of his torch was making an ellipse of brightness on the table. In the centre of the table there was an open book. He went over to it. He could see the thin, spidery writing on the yellowing pages. It was Lovebody's Journal, the original, not the printed copy, and above it the glass-fronted bookcase was open, the key still in the lock. In the margin Septimus could see the pencil marks that had guided the Archdeacon's reading. 'Primrose screamed as he died. I had not thought of that.'

He left the book where it was and went out of the library, closing the door softly behind him. He stood for a moment by the base of one of the pillars, gazing round the nave, listening, searching the darkness. For what seemed a long time there was nothing, but then he saw a flash of light by the door at the top of the Petersteps, as if someone were having to use a torch to negotiate the door. He went quietly between the pews and down the north aisle. Through the glass of the door he could see a glimmer of light at the top of the Petersteps. It flickered and faded, glancing over the stone walls. He watched. The light was not moving down the steps. Whoever was carrying the torch was doing something at the top of the steps by Primrose's grave. Cautiously he inched the door open and slid through. The air blew cold up the Petersteps.

The light was coming from Primrose's open grave. He stepped to the barrier and looked down into the hole. There was a man, a bearded man with a torch. He had removed the sacks covering the coffin lid, and Septimus could see his hand white in the torchlight as he brushed earth from the inscription. He could hear the excited hiss of the man's breathing as the lettering came into view.

R.I.P.
Hezekiah Primrose
1737 - 1772

Septimus weighed the heavy torch in his hand as if it were a truncheon and spoke with an almost conscious parody of his days as a constable with the Metropolitan Police.

'Now then. And what do you think you're up to?'

The intruder gasped. 'Screamed' might be a better word. The torchlight flashed momentarily across Septimus, and then with a cursing, a patter of earth and a clatter of flagstones, the intruder jumped out of the hole on the far side and ran up the circular stairs.

Septimus used an unclerical word, vaulted lightly over the barrier, and landed heavily in the hole. It wasn't much use, he thought bitterly as he felt the jarring pain in his knee, having been a champion athlete for the police if you were talking about thirty-five years ago. He clambered clumsily out of the hole, wincing, using more unclerical language, and went to the bottom of the circular stairs. The intruder was out of sight and sound, and Septimus was about to follow when he had a better idea. 'Septimus,' he was thinking, 'you're a respectable country clergyman. You're too old for pounding after villains.' As he was thinking, so he was busy with the door. The workmen had left the key in it, and by moving two or three paving stones and pushing a quantity of earth into the grave, he was able to close and lock the door.

He went back down the nave to the room under the organ and extracted from his pack a length of cord and a can of beer. He tied the cord between the posts at the bottom of the organ steps, and then stood in the shadows, waiting, drinking the beer straight from the can.

There were only two ways down from the clerestory. One was locked, and this was the other.

Ten minutes later he heard a click and rattle from far down the aisle. He raised his can of beer in noiseless salute. The intruder had tried the door at the bottom of the circular stairs. 'May the ghost of Hezekiah rise and haunt you,' he murmured.

Ten minutes passed and then Septimus saw the flicker of the torch against the bottom of the west window. The intruder was going round the clerestory, but in the wrong direction. He would have to make a circuit of the whole Minster before he reached the steps by the organ. Septimus walked out into the choir to the top of the chancel steps the better to watch the intruder's progress. And as he stood there, the organ started to play. The music was soft at first, muzzy and distant, and there was a pronounced echo to it as if it did not belong in the Minster. It was growing louder all the time,

55.

more sure of itself. Septimus turned to go to the controls of the public address system but as he did so he heard the clatter of footsteps on stone and saw the torch moving jerkily and far too fast down the clerestory on the south side. The fool of an intruder was running. With sudden insight Septimus realized that the bearded man was terrified. Surprised in the grave, trapped in the clerestory, and now he heard the weird music coming from nowhere. It was hardly surprising – Septimus had felt a chill of fear when that weird noise had started. But the clerestory balustrade was low, the walkway of uneven width and no place for running even in daylight, and Septimus had no desire to see the affair end in a real tragedy with the bearded man falling into the nave.

'Don't!' he shouted. 'Don't!' But his sudden shout echoing and bellowing down the nave, with the music seeming to mock it, only made matters worse. To the intruder it sounded like another ingredient in the haunting. There was a thump and a sharp cry from the clerestory and the torch described a spinning arc and crashed to the nave floor. For a heart-stopping second Septimus thought the worst had happened. But it had only been the torch, not the man. Evidently he had run into something in his panic. 'Serve him right,' thought Septimus callously. 'If he's knocked himself out, so much the better. Keep him quiet for ten minutes.'

The music was filling the nave with sound now, a gay triumphant tune which sounded as if it should be played on horns. The very gaiety of it coming from nowhere made it sound more ghostly. Septimus went down the centre aisle trying to gauge whether it was coming from the speakers on the pillars, but they were too high, and it was not possible to tell. He ran back to the control panel and heedless of the Archdeacon's threads swung the doors open. He flicked switches and opened faders, but it made no difference to the music. He ran to the steps leading up to the organ loft, tripped over his own cord and fell headlong, cursing. He extricated himself and went up the steps. The organ loft was dark, the keyboard closed, the books and music as they had been earlier in the day. He went a little way along the clerestory and leaned over the balustrade stretching his head down to one of the speakers. But it was no use. The speaker was too far away. He stood up, cursing impotently, feeling every sort of a fool. As he stood, so the music faded away and the building was silent as it had been before.

He walked slowly back to the organ and down the stairs. This time he remembered to undo his cord before he went headlong over it. He retied the cord behind him and went and stood in the shadow by a pillar. He was feeling irritated now. First round to the ghost. He had been present for a haunting session, and he had discovered precisely nothing. That was not entirely true. At least he knew that the music was not controlled from the panel under the organ, and that was something gained. Meantime there was the black-bearded gent in the clerestory. Septimus decided to give him a quarter of an hour before going up to see if he had broken his neck. In his present mood, he acknowledged savagely, he rather hoped the man *had* broken his neck. Well . . . not his neck, but it would be only justice if he had done himself an injury.

It was about twelve minutes before Septimus heard cautious footsteps on the stairs. He tensed in the shadows, waiting, grinning a little as he realized that he was largely concerned that the bearded man should not in fact break his neck when he went headlong over the cord.

A moment later he saw a movement in the shadows at the bottom of the stairs. There was a stifled cry as the man's foot caught in the cord. Septimus was ready. He ran forward, arms outstretched to catch the flying figure, to break the man's fall before he hit the unsympathetic tiles. He mistimed it slightly and the man's head hit him like a battering ram in the midriff. Septimus collapsed with a hiccough of suddenly expelled breath, and the two of them rolled together on the floor, Septimus winded and in considerable pain, the intruder once again terrified.

Despite the agony of his solar plexus, Septimus managed to get the man's arm behind his back in a half nelson. He stumbled to his feet, dragging the intruder up. 'Got you, my lad,' he wheezed, for all the world like a police constable in a pub brawl. The bearded man said nothing but he suddenly turned so far as the arm hold would allow and launched a vicious kick in the general direction of Septimus's shin. The kick connected. Septimus yelped with pain and lost his grip on the man's arm. The man turned to bolt and at that moment Septimus lost his temper entirely. It was a rare event, which was just as well because despite his age he was still a powerful man and he had once been a not inconsiderable middle-weight boxer. He clenched his big fist and launched a massive punch at the intruder's chin. Had it connected, that would certainly have been the end of the fight, and the intruder would probably have had a broken jaw beneath his black beard. As it was, and perhaps not surprisingly, the punch went high and landed on the cheekbone, sending a jar down Septimus's forearm. The intruder crashed to the tiles, stunned, and Septimus lost sight of him in the darkness. He stood a moment, his chest heaving, the agony in his midriff only a little abated. His opponent was very still, somewhere in the shadows of the floor. Presumably he was unconscious. Septimus's anger ebbed away. He should not have hit the young man like that. It was really most unprofessional – the sort of thing that brought the police into disrepute. He could hear himself lecturing young constables on the absolute necessity of keeping one's temper.

He took two steps forward, his ankle was grabbed and his feet were pulled from beneath him. He never knew what he hit his head on, but when he came back to consciousness he was lying on the tiles beneath the organ and he was alone in the Minster. The only consolation he could think of as he sat up, groaning and rubbing the back of his head, was that in the morning the bearded young man would have the best black eye in East Anglia. Bruised and irritable, he went to bed, but not before he had replaced the Archdeacon's threads on the doors of the control panel.

He awoke next morning conscious that there was something niggling at his mind. He was stiff, but nothing worse from the previous night's fracas. He clambered out of his sleeping bag, rubbing his unshaven chin, and went into the choir where the dawn was beginning to struggle through the east window. Then he remembered the library and Lovebody's Journal lying on the table. He went across. All was as he had left it in the library – except that Lovebody's Journal had disappeared from the table. Its place in the glass-fronted bookcase was empty, but the bookcase had been locked and the key put back in the drawer.

6 Straws in the Wind

Septimus put down his teacup and gazed out of the bow window of the Dean's study.

'Certainly,' said the Dean, 'there's a full account of Primrose's murder. I'm surprised the Archdeacon did not tell you. There's a copy of it bound in the back of the manuscript of Lovebody's Journal.'

Septimus was surprised. But not – he reflected – half as surprised as the Dean would be if he knew that the Journal was missing from the Chapter library. Septimus supposed it was a valuable book, and his police instincts cried out that something should be done about the theft. But life was already complicated enough without having the local C.I.D. tramping round the Minster in regulation boots. Anyway, he had a hunch about the Journal.

'What sort of an account?' he asked.

'Oh, the typical eighteenth-century thing,' said the Dean. 'Full confession. Account of the trial and execution. Printed in broadsheet and sold by chapmen and ballad-mongers. It was common practice at the time.'

'Sort of eighteenth-century horror comic,' said Septimus.

'Yes,' said the Dean, 'I've got a copy of it somewhere.' He went across the study and rummaged in one of his bookcases. 'Picked it up in the Turl nearly half a century ago. That sort of thing was cheaper then. Worth its weight in gold now, I suppose. Ah. Here we are.'

He brought a slim volume, bound in leather, to the window, and Septimus stood beside him as he turned the badly printed pages.

'Account of the late Apparitions ... The Ballad of Tim Oakley ... Confessions of Mary Withers. Taken up as a Witch ... Ah. Here we are. Account of the Most Horrible Murder of Hezekiah Primrose Esquire, late of the County of Norfolk. With the Trial of Captain John Jancey, His Confession, Gallows Speech, and Execution ... Read it for yourself,' said the Dean, handing the book to Septimus.

Septimus read in silence, finding it a professionally interesting document. It was a curious mixture of extracts from the court proceedings, sensational details and the conventional piety of the day.

The trial had really hinged on two points: the circumstantial evidence about the affair between Primrose and Janet Jancey; and to Septimus, the much more damning evidence of the first lieutenant of the *Pelican* that the knife which killed Primrose belonged to John Jancey.

Jancey's 'Gallows Speech' contained a fairly full account of what had happened on that eventful night. It was much given to pious ejaculations and phrases that no seaman would ever have used, so that Septimus guessed that it had been compiled by the writer of the broadsheet after Jancey had been helped out of this world by the hangman. Even so, stripped of padding, it squared with what Septimus already knew of the affair.

The brig *Pelican* had come home after ten months surveying along the west coast of Africa. There had been a thick mist off shore, so Jancey had anchored in the approaches to the harbour. In the late afternoon of the 14th August the mist had cleared. Jancey had weighed anchor and started to come in, knowing that he would make harbour after nightfall, but trusting to the Lantern for the final, difficult approach. At the critical moment the light had failed. By what must have been superb seamanship, Jancey had brought the brig in. In a towering passion because of the light, he had gone ashore, only to find his wife in a state of near hysteria. He had discovered that she was pregnant, extracted from her the name of the man responsible, and taking a lantern, had gone off in search of Primrose.

At this point there was a curious insertion into the narrative which, for Septimus with his knowledge of court proceedings, bore the hallmark of actuality. A man called Foster had been constable of the watch that night. He gave evidence that he had met Captain Jancey outside Primrose's house. 'He was in a great rage and shouted at me, accusing me of hiding Mr Primrose. So I said, "If it's Mr Primrose you want, you'll find him in the Minster, for I heard the organ playing not five minutes gone." So I bid him a civil good night, suggesting he go to his bed where all honest folk were at that hour.'

But Jancey had not gone to his bed. He had gone to the door at the bottom of the Petersteps, and hearing the organ still playing, had smashed it open with his foot. He had gone up the circular stairway into the clerestory. He had surprised Primrose at his keyboard and after a brief struggle had stabbed him to death. Then he had stumbled back the way he had come, so down to the harbour and aboard his ship.

Septimus closed the book. 'And there's a copy of this in the back of Lovebody's Journal?' he said.

'Yes,' said the Dean.

Deep in thought, Septimus gazed down Chandlers Way. Why had the Archdeacon not told him about the broadsheet? A pure oversight? Or could there be a more sinister motive?

There was a motor cyclist turning into the car park at the

bottom of the hill. Half Septimus's mind identified the motor cyclist as Norman Barnes, the other half was wondering who had stolen Lovebody's Journal from the library.

The Minster clock chimed the half hour and Septimus got to his feet.

'Thank you, Dean,' he said. 'That's been very helpful. But I must go. I've got something I must do before the shops close.'

'Are you any nearer a solution?' asked the Dean as he led the way through the hall.

Septimus shook his head. 'One or two ideas. But that's all.' He paused on the doorstep. 'There's one thing I'd be glad if you'd do for me.'

'Anything I can,' said the Dean.

'Could you compile a list of all the full-time cathedral staff – clergy and lay – with the dates when they came?'

'Gladly,' said the Dean. 'Let you have it tomorrow.'

Septimus set off in the direction of the Peterport, but he had hardly taken a dozen steps when the Deanery door crashed open again and Alisdair Cameron came pelting after him.

'Septimus! Septimus!' He was wildly excited and out of breath. 'It's started again. The organ music. I was in my room and I heard it. The same music I heard that night.'

'In the middle of the afternoon?' said Septimus.

'Come on!' said Alisdair and led the way to the Minster.

It *was* the same piece of music – gay, lilting, as if it ought to be played on horns, but it did not echo, and there was nothing sinister about it. Indeed, the holidaymakers wandering about the great building were taking it as a matter of course – a proper part of the Minster scene, like the arches and the tombs. Someone was playing the organ – it was what people did in cathedrals.

Septimus and Alisdair hurried down the aisle. They passed

Ted Barnes going the other way and carrying a bag of tools, but he merely smiled at them as he passed. Obviously Ted had not recognized the piece of music that was being played.

The light in the organ loft was on. Septimus led the way up the steps and opened the half door at the top. Berwick was sitting on the stool, his long fingers sidling over the keys, his face yellow in the soft light. He half turned as they came in, smiling in his superior way. He brought the piece to a peeling, triumphant conclusion, and then the sounds died until there was only the gentle hum of the organ motor.

'Ah. The reverend Chief Inspector,' said Berwick. He twitched the piece of music off the rest and handed it to Septimus.

'I thought I'd heard it before,' he said. 'I spent a dusty morning in the pre-historic section of the music library. And behold! Virtue is its own reward.'

It was a piece of manuscript music, the paper brittle and cracked, the ink brown with age. In a bold cursive script it was headed 'Suite for Janet' by Hezekiah Primrose.

Septimus turned the crumbling pages. He could read neither the music nor the notes in the margin, which were written – presumably – by Primrose himself. There were other notes, much more modern, written in pencil.

'What do you make of these?' asked Septimus, pointing to the pencil notes.

Berwick shrugged. 'They're the sort of notes I might make if I proposed to play the piece seriously. They're initialled S.T. I expect he was another of my illustrious predecessors. Primrose wrote the piece very much for his own organ, and of course you have to adapt – the instrument's changed a bit since his day.'

Septimus looked at his watch. 'Can I keep this music for a bit, Mr Berwick?'

'My pleasure,' said the organist and turned back to his keyboard.

Septimus and Alisdair came down the organ stairs to the strains of Bach.

Harry Tulloch and Ted Barnes were standing together at the bottom of the chancel steps, the visitors drifting round them as if they were a couple of rocks in the middle of a sluggish river. Harry had a vacuum-cleaner in his hands, Ted was clutching his bag of tools. There was a frown on Harry's face which cleared as he saw Septimus. 'Major!' he said. 'Just the man. Ted's found something that you ought to see.' He looked round at the visitors. 'But not here. Let's go to my cubby-hole. Well . . . yes, all right, Master Alisdair, you can come. But mum's the word, my lad.'

The four of them squeezed into the cluttered little room and Harry closed the door. 'Now then, Ted,' he said in a conspiratorial whisper, 'show the Major.' Ted opened his tool bag and brought out a book, a big book bound in red leather which Septimus recognized even before Ted handed it to him. It was Canon Lovebody's Journal.

'Where did you find it?' Septimus asked, riffling the pages.

'Well, that's the funny thing,' said Ted. 'I bin up to check the Lantern. Do it every month. That was where I was off to when you came into the Minster, Mr Treloar. Well. I changed the bulb. I do that every three months, regular. It being important that the Lantern don't go out. Then I wanted to test the bulb, see? Well. The switch is behind the door. So I had to close the door. That book. It was on the floor behind the door.'

'You know what it is?' asked Septimus.

'Ah. It's old Lovebody's diary. You and Himmler were looking at it yesterday in the library.'

'What I want to know is,' said Harry, 'how did it get into

the flippin' Lantern? His Nibs would do his nut if he knew – begging your pardon, Master Alisdair. But he would, you know. So don't you go telling him.'

'I'd like to know the answer to that myself,' said Septimus. He was thinking furiously. This discovery simply did not fit with any idea of a haunting. Ghosts did not carry books and leave them behind doors. It was like a piece out of the wrong jigsaw puzzle. He handed the book to Harry. 'Better put it back in the library,' he said. 'And Harry, I should take those keys out of the drawer. Tell the librarian to keep them somewhere else.'

'Well, as to telling the Chapter librarian . . .' said Harry. 'But you're right, Major. I'll think of something. Only he isn't the sort of chap you can actually tell things to, if you see what I mean. And if the actress didn't say that about the bishop – she should have done.'

7   Two Bottles of Gin

Septimus arrived at Sophia Wenlock's bookshop just as Mrs Wenlock herself was locking the door. She looked to him more like a fishwife than a bookseller.

'Mrs Wenlock?' said Septimus.

She turned and peered at him through pebble glasses so thick that they hid her eyes. The glasses looked like two mountain pools in the hilly contours of her face.

'That's me. I'm Sophie Wenlock. And you'll be the Reverend Treloar, duckie.'

Septimus was startled. Not simply because she knew his name, but much more by her voice. He had been expecting a squeak from all that fat – like a pig. But her voice was deep, a bass voice, almost a man's voice.

'Yes,' he said, mentally apologizing for expecting her to sound like a pig.

'Yes. I'm Treloar. I wanted to talk to you.'

'About Hezekiah Primrose's spirit, isn't it? Well, you'd better come back into the shop.' She unlocked the door and led the way inside.

The shop was pokey. It was dusty from the books which were stacked from floor to ceiling so that the planks bowed under their weight. There were books everywhere – in cases, piled in corners, heaped on rickety tables. There were prints and old records where there were not books, so that there was hardly room for customers, let alone for the considerable form of Mrs Wenlock. A tiny desk was squeezed somehow into one corner. Septimus never saw how she did it, but by some feat of magic Mrs Wenlock managed to get herself behind the desk. When she sat down she so dominated the desk that it looked like a tray perched on her ample lap. Her spectacles flashed in the light of the single, unshaded bulb.

'Sit down, Reverend. Make yourself at home.' Septimus looked wildly round and then removed a pile of records from an old kitchen chair.

'Now,' he said severely, 'what's all this about ghosts in the Minster, Mrs Wenlock?'

'Why! It's all over the town, Reverend. I'd have thought you'd have known that. You having been a Chief Inspector before you were a Reverend. *And* engaged by the Dean himself, all special to investigate the haunting.'

'Who said I'd come to investigate a haunting?'

Mrs Wenlock looked totally astonished.

'Well of course you have. What are you doing here if you aren't investigating? Have you come to buy a dirty book?'

Septimus did not feel he was doing very well. Cross-questioning Mrs Wenlock was going to be a bit like dealing with a feather bed. You thumped it down in one place and it bulged out in another. He tried a new tack.

'What are they saying is happening? In the town, that is.'

'Bless you Reverend, nothing's happening in the town so far as I know. Though they do say that Dessie West's baby – the one with the flaxen hair . . .'

Septimus cut across the piece of gossip. 'No. You misunderstand me. What are they saying about this supposed haunting in the Minster?'

'Why! You know as well as I do, Reverend. It's all over the town. Nellie, she's the barmaid in the Master Mariner, and no better than she should be, she was saying only last night that it was all happening just as you might expect.'

'But what?' asked Septimus desperately. 'What is supposed to be happening?'

'Oh, hoity-toity,' she said, 'you needn't sell your rag to the man with the little red eyes. Even if you are a Reverend. But I'll tell you what's happening. Lights in the clerestory. And the organ playing when Mr Berwick's plunged fathoms deep in his bed.' She stopped talking for a long moment and the pebble glasses were still. Septimus could only conclude that she was staring at him. When she spoke again her deep voice had taken on a sombre tone so that Septimus was suddenly reminded that once she had been a medium. Quite suddenly she seemed to be a different sort of person.

'There are no living hands on those keys. They're the hands of the dead.'

'Whose hands?' asked Septimus. She laughed so that her flesh shook and the momentary sombreness was broken.

'Why! Hezekiah Primrose, of course. Him they dug up yesterday morning.'

'And who says it's Hezekiah Primrose?'

Once again she was still and the deeper tone thrilled in her voice.

'I do. Him with his grave opened this first time in two hundred years, and nigh on the anniversary of his death. That day when John Jancey walked in the clerestory, a lantern in his hand, a knife at his belt. They sleep lightly, Mr Treloar, the unquiet dead – even after two hundred years.'

Septimus refused to be impressed. 'The Account of the Most Horrible Murder of Hezekiah Primrose Esquire . . .' he quoted. 'And where did *you* see a copy of the broadsheet, Mrs Wenlock?'

This time she laughed uproariously, setting the little desk dancing on her knees.

'You're a one,' she said, 'indeed you are. Ah well! You

must allow me the little tricks of my trade, Reverend. I was a medium once, you know. I could teach you all about ectoplasm, spirit-writing and emanations. If you had a mind to learn. And talking about spirits, I generally have a little something just after I've closed the shop. The dust from the books gets into your tubes so. Have a little something with me, Reverend.'

Before Septimus could answer, from a cupboard over her head she produced a bottle of gin, two tumblers and a glass of water.

Septimus waited while she poured drinks – big drinks with much gin and little water.

'Your health, Mrs Wenlock,' he said. 'Where did you read the broadsheet about the murder?'

'I had a copy in the shop, Reverend. Ten years ago. Being local stuff, I read it before I sold it. Not that I read the stock usually. Too much like a greengrocer eating his own onions. Sold it to the Minster library. They had it bound in the back of old Lovebody's diary – or so the librarian told me when he came in about an illustrated edition of the *Decameron*.'

She took a gulp at her gin. 'He was a naughty old man, that librarian,' she said reminiscently.

Septimus did not reply at once. Why had the Archdeacon not mentioned the existence of the broadsheet? And how had Lovebody's Journal got into the Lantern? He came back to the present. Mrs Wenlock was pouring herself another large gin and still talking.

'. . . as I've often found, clergymen is good customers for what you might call the Slightly Off. Cambridge blue rather than Oxford blue if you take my meaning. By the way, Reverend, I suppose you'd not be interested in an illustrated edition of the *Kama Sutra*?' Her pebble spectacles had slipped down her nose and she looked at him over the lenses and over her raised glass of gin. Septimus shook his head.

'Ah, well . . . But then you've been a policeman and that makes a difference. Never get policemen buying the porn – except in the line of duty as you might say. Least, they *say* it's duty . . . But it's the narrow ways as makes a bit of lush pasture attractive. 'Course you can't always tell.'

She took a swig at her glass, making herself cough. 'Now you take the Venerable Jenkins. He was in here the other day looking at a Catullus. Thought he was fair game, I did. So I offered *him* the *Kama Sutra*. Proper hoity-toity he was. Said he didn't paddle in filth. Least, I think he said paddle though it might have been peddle. But then the Venerable Jenkins never did like me. Not since we fell out over a bit of spirit rapping. And that was fifteen years since. How time flies as the monkey said when it threw the clock at the missionary. Have another gin.'

She was already pouring one for herself, and she gave Septimus no time to refuse.

'Tell me . . .' he murmured, his eyebrows rising as the gin rose in his glass. 'Whoa! That's enough, Mrs Wenlock.'

'Tell you what?' she asked. 'About the monkey and the missionary?'

'No. About the Archdeacon.'

It was some moments before she replied. 'It's a funny thing, Reverend,' she said at last, 'that spirit rapping may have been me. I'll not say it wasn't. But there was more to it than that. Nine tenths fiddle, as my old man used to say. But there's always the other tenth.' She fell silent again.

'Tell me,' said Septimus.

'Fifteen years since,' she murmured. 'My Harry was still alive. Kept the pub at Salwarpe Saint Anthony, we did. The Jolly Waggoner. Jenkins, he was the Vicar of the Salwarpes. Saint Anthony, Saint Benet and Saint Clare, that is. Handsome is as handsome does, I say. And that Jenkins, right old curmudgeon he was. Steal the halfpennies out of the baby's money-box to put on his granny's eyelids. Well. I did a bit in the medium line. There weren't no harm in it, not really. Started as a bit of fun. I knew all about the folks in the village, and there was always the gossip in the bar if you kept your ears open. I learned a few of the tricks too – like how to do spirit rappings. Do you know how to do spirit rappings, Reverend?'

'With a box strapped to your knees,' said Septimus. 'I once knew a jewel thief who used it to pinch a diamond brooch from a duchess.' He had not intended to add the anecdote, but he had already drunk more gin than he liked.

'You don't say!' said Mrs Wenlock admiringly. 'Now how did he do that?'

Septimus cursed himself silently for the digression.

'He went into a trance and rapped away like mad, telling the duchess all about her brother who'd been killed in the War. She was so taken up thinking about her brother that she never noticed him whip the brooch. He put it in the box before he came out of his trance and they put the lights on. But you were telling me about the Archdeacon.'

Mrs Wenlock took no notice. 'He'd be wearing trousers,' she said. 'What did he do? Roll 'em up from the bottom? Or go down from the top?' She giggled girlishly.

'He wore a long robe,' said Septimus desperately. 'Now what about the Archdeacon?'

'But didn't it rattle in the box?'

'He had it padded,' Septimus said. He anticipated the next question. 'And he'd cut a hole in the lid so he could slip it in without having to open the box. Now I'm longing to hear about the Archdeacon?'

'Very ingenious,' she said, picking up the gin bottle. 'Well I do declare, Reverend. It's empty. No. I can't tell you that harrowing story, not without a little something to keep me going. If you care to escort me to the Master Mariner where I generally go about this time, I shall be most happy to unburden myself upon you.'

'No,' thought Septimus wildly. 'No. Not the Master Mariner. They'd unfrock me.' He struggled to keep his face straight at the thought of what the Archdeacon would say. Anyway, he would never get the rest of the story once Ma Wenlock was loose in a pub. He rose to his feet, fumbling for his wallet.

'Mrs Wenlock, you must allow me. I positively insist. I am so enjoying our little *tête-a-tête*. I haven't enjoyed myself so much since I last took a lady police sergeant to the – the Chelsea Arts Ball. And as I appear to have drunk all your gin you must allow me to make good the deficiency. Indeed, dear lady, I positively insist. Now you just wait there. I shall be back in five minutes.' He walked toward the door, wondering wryly what Minster Saint Peter would say when word got round that he had rushed into the Master Mariner demanding a bottle of gin about ten minutes after the pub opened. But Mrs Wenlock would not let him go. She called him 'duckie reverend' and pinched his cheek and took the banknotes out of his nerveless hand.

'Can't have you pubbing in your canonicals,' she said, going to the door and looking out into the alley. 'Timmie!' she shrieked, 'Timmie Huxtable! Come here this minute. Auntie Sophie wants you.' In a moment a grubby urchin appeared. She gave him instructions and Septimus's money and then shut the shop door. 'Little Timmie,' she said. 'He runs all my errands.' Septimus, whose head was beginning to ache, could guess the destination of most of Timmie's errands. He tried to steer Mrs Wenlock back to the subject of the Archdeacon, but she would have none of it until Timmie returned with the bottle of gin. Septimus managed to get to the door before his hostess. He took the gin and the change, tipped Timmie, and ignored the 'Cor!' with which the urchin greeted his clerical collar.

'Now,' he said firmly as he shut the door, 'you have played hostess. I shall play host.' If he was not to end up unconscious on the floor, he simply had to keep control of the gin bottle.

It took him over an hour and most of the gin to get the story out of her. Whether from a congenital inability to stick to the subject, or whether from a reluctance to talk about that particular subject, he could not tell. She kept wandering off into endless digressions, like a cow in a country lane, and he had to guide her back on course, pricking her with questions. He learned a great deal about her. About her childhood as the daughter of a Lowestoft fisherman. About her family – three sons, one in the butchery business, one at sea, one dead. About Harry Wenlock, and how he had broken his neck by falling down the cellar steps at the Jolly Waggoner. Harry was good for ten minutes – 'Sober he was, Reverend. Sober as I'm sitting here.'

Slowly the story came out. In Salwarpe Saint Anthony there had been a man called Eddie whose wife, Mary, had died. In his loneliness Eddie had turned to Mrs Wenlock. She, with a curious mixture of compassion and trickery, had given him what comfort she could through her faked séances. Septimus was beginning to realize that the issues – even in crooked mediumship – were not the straight blacks and whites of the Archdeacon.

'Well, of course I knew all about the family. So I was able to get in touch with her as you might say.' She took a swig of gin. 'And oh, Reverend! The difference to that man! He went back to his smallholding. Humming like a lark, he was.' But the Reverend Aloysius Jenkins had got wind of the matter.

'Preached a sermon, he did. All about the Witch of Endor.

Well. I'm no witch, Reverend, whatever else I am. As my Harry told him. Threatened to knock him down, and him in his canonicals just like you.' The upshot had been that the vicar had come uninvited to one of the séances at the Jolly Waggoner and had exposed Sophia Wenlock as a fraud. 'Found the hooks for the table levitation, he did, and the rapping box. Though as God's my witness, I never used them that night. But that was the end of me.' She suddenly burst into tears, rivulets of salt water coursing down her fat cheeks.

Septimus was puzzled. Was it just the gin, or was there some deeper reason for her grief?

'Why are you crying?' he asked gently, offering her a handkerchief.

She sniffed, taking the handkerchief, mopping her cheeks.

'It's funny, really. You see Reverend, that night were part of the tenth that isn't a fiddle. I didn't use no tricks that night, and I didn't know what I'd said. But I told Eddie things . . .' She paused, remembering.

'What things?'

'Things that only his Mary could have known. Eddie knew it and I knew it. And Jenkins knew it after. But it didn't make no difference. He branded me for the Witch of Endor.'

'I see,' said Septimus. 'Thank you for telling me, Mrs Hemlock. And I'm sorry if it distressed you.'

He got up uncertainly. There seemed to be two doors, and he had to concentrate on his eyes to reduce the number. He succeeded and made a determinedly straight course for it. At the door he paused.

'Mrs Fetlock, he said soberly. 'Eddie. Eddie what?'

She sniffed. 'I wasn't going to tell you. It being a personal matter. But Mr Treloar, you're a gentleman, even if you are a reverend. Eddie Barnes. Him that's verger up at the Minster.'

'Ted Barnes,' said Septimus. 'Well, I'm blessed.' He stepped out into the alley and closed the door behind him.

'I see,' he said to a passing cat. The cat took no notice. He shook his finger after the cat. 'You don't see, Septimus Treloar. Nor are you blessed. You're drunk.' He turned up the alley.

'Onward Christian soldiers,' he murmured.

He marched in what he hoped was a reasonably straight line through the market-place and up Chandlers Way. The Archdeacon was coming out of his gate.

'Christian soldiers keep your column of file,' Septimus murmured to himself. And then out loud and, he hoped, obsequiously, 'Good evening, Archdeacon.'

'Good evening, Treloar. Going to the Minster at this time of night?'

'Yes,' said Septimus, 'I have an appointment – with the Witch of Endor.'

He had not intended to say the last bit out loud.

'I beg your pardon!' said the Archdeacon.

'Granted,' said Septimus over his shoulder, and marched in a gentle curve up the cobbled hill.

He never knew whether or not the organ played that night, or whether there were any intruders. He awoke at six in the morning with a splitting headache and a mouth like a crocodile's armpit. He groaned as he opened his eyes. He staggered out of his sleeping bag and peered lugubriously out from under the organ. 'I doubt if I shall live,' he said, 'but at least no one pinched the Minster while I slept it off.'

8　The Best Black Eye in East Anglia

Because of the gin Septimus was late getting up, and he was still rolling up his sleeping bag when Harry Tulloch stuck his head round the door of the room beneath the organ.

'Major, you've been rumbled, and His Nibs wants to see you before you go home.' Septimus groaned.

'Ah. Colonel's defaulters for you, Major. I saw you last night. So did Himmler. He went straight to the Dean.' Septimus groaned again.

'Wasn't I walking very straight, Harry?'

'Well not what I'd call straight, as the actress said to the bishop. But cheer up Major. I'll believe it was in the line of duty, even if no one else will.'

'It was duty,' said Septimus. 'I was entertaining Ma Wenlock.'

'Oh, her. That's duty right enough.'

The Dean greeted Septimus with an amused grin. 'The b-black coffee is ready, my dear Septimus. And when you are feeling strong enough I have something to show you.' Septimus accepted the coffee gratefully.

'You're not proposing to have me unfrocked for being drunk and disorderly on Chapter property?' he asked.

'Were you disorderly as well?' asked the Dean. 'The Archdeacon merely said you had told him that you had an appointment with the Witch of Endor.'

'Did I now?' said Septimus, startled.

'The Archdeacon also said you were sleeping in the Minster. He was quite huffy about it. He made it sound as if you were a vagrant. He told me he was quite capable of dealing with any hauntings, faked or otherwise.'

'And so?' said Septimus.

'So I told him I was responsible for the Minster and I'd asked you to investigate, and if you were sleeping in the Minster, it was with my permission.'

'Thank you, sir.'

The Dean smiled. 'So much for Aloysius. And if your head aches, my dear Septimus, you've only yourself to blame . . . Now look at this morning's local paper.' He passed across a copy of *The Minster Saint Peter and North Norfolk Advertiser*. On the front page there was a staring headline. 'Minster Haunted? Ghost of Former Organist.'

Septimus read the account. It was well informed and reasonably accurate. He could detect the voice of Sophia Wenlock in one or two places. What bothered him about it was the firm way the playing of the organ and the light in the clerestory had been linked with the uncovering of Primrose's coffin. After all, that had only just happened, and local papers did not normally work to very tight deadlines.

'What are you going to do?' he asked. 'You'll have all the national dailies breathing down your neck in a brace of shakes.'

'I know,' said the Dean grimly. 'I'm seeing the editor at ten. I thought you might like to come. At least I can try to beat the stable boy – even if the horse is gone.'

The office of the *Advertiser* was along the seafront, opposite the main bathing beach. The two priests, conspicuous in their clerical grey, threaded their way among the gaily dressed holidaymakers, past the shops selling rock and buckets and spades, past the chalked notices about trips round the bay, and so up the steps at the front of the unimpressive building.

Inside the glazed door was a small railed-off space in one big office. There was a counter immediately in front of the door, and beyond it and on either side, desks and typewriters, people working in a welter of paper and an atmosphere of tobacco smoke and the smell of printer's ink.

A girl sitting at the counter looked up inquiringly as they came in.

'I have an appointment with Mr Edwards,' said the Dean frostily.

Septimus's eye fell on a young man sitting at a desk to the left of the counter. The young man had curly black hair, a black beard and a very black eye. Septimus touched the Dean's elbow. 'Excuse me, Dean,' he said, 'I'll leave you to deal with the stable door. I've got a date with the horse thief.' He leaned on the rail, his face close to the young man's ear. 'Young man,' he said. 'You will take me out and buy me a cup of coffee. Otherwise I shall black the other eye.' Astonishment, fear, and then amusement chased one another across the man's face. 'Delighted,' he said.

The Yachtsman's Café, three doors along the front from the newspaper office, was nearly empty. They went to a table by the window looking across the road to the beach where holiday families were beginning to set up camp with rugs and picnic baskets and windbreaks.

Septimus waited until the young man had ordered coffee, then he stuck out his hand. 'Septimus Treloar,' he said. 'What's your name, my lad? And what do you mean by it?'

'John Jones,' said the other, taking the proffered hand, 'and I meant a cracking good story by it. Not every day that the cub reporter makes the main story on the front page.

Did you enjoy my story, Mr Treloar? We've already had the *Mirror* on the blower.'

'And now you've got the Dean on your back,' growled Septimus, accepting coffee. 'Don't trifle with me, young man. I'm old and decayed and bad-tempered. How did you do it?'

'Easy. I hid in the Lady Chapel until they'd locked up.'

'Why?'

'I'd heard old Ma Wenlock in the Master Mariner. She was talking about the Minster being haunted. I thought there might be a paragraph in it. Not a front page spread.' He grinned appreciatively.

'Don't look so pleased with yourself, or I will black the other eye,' Septimus said. John Jones continued to grin. He was warming to this large and elderly parson with the face like a bus smash.

'Now, my lad, you tell me exactly what you did after you came out of that Lady Chapel.'

'I went down the north side and hid behind a tomb near the top of the Petersteps.'

'Did you see me?'

John Jones shook his head. 'Not till you caught me in the grave. I heard you, though. "I am the ghost of Septimus Treloar. The Venerable Aloysius Jenkins murdered me." I heard you say that. Wondered what the devil was going on.'

Septimus was slightly mollified, despite having been over-heard in the piece of nonsense with the tape recorder. At least he could still move quietly and inconspicuously.

'And you saw no one else but me?' he asked.

'No. I heard someone come in and go out – that was before you spoke, though.'

Septimus nodded. That would have been the Archdeacon setting up his traps.

'You didn't see who it was?' he asked.

'No. I took a peep from behind the tomb. But I didn't see anyone.'

'Then what happened?'

'Well I stayed behind the tomb for a long time. Then I went and climbed into the grave to see whose coffin it was. You know the rest.' Mr Jones put down his coffee cup. 'I've never been so scared in all my life as when you caught me in that grave. Except a few minutes later when the organ started to play and you shouted at me. I suppose it *was you?*'

Septimus nodded abstractedly. Apparently Jones had been nowhere near the Chapter library. Who then had removed Lovebody's Journal?

'Yes. It was me that shouted,' he said. 'I was afraid you were going to fall.'

'It sounded horrible,' said Jones seriously. 'For a moment I thought you were Primrose and Jancey was sticking his knife in your back. Then I ran into a pillar and laid myself out.'

'Serves you right,' said Septimus unsympathetically. 'You shouldn't trespass in other people's clerestories. But – look – I want to establish something important. You never went into the south aisle at all? You didn't go into the Chapter library?'

'No,' the reporter replied. 'Honour bright. I don't even know where it is. Why? Was there another story I missed? If you tell me now I could make next week's front page as well.'

Septimus scowled. 'My lad, when the Dean's finished with your editor, you'll be lucky if you can make the obituaries.'

'You heartless old man,' replied the unrepentant Mr Jones.

Septimus reported back to the Deanery to find the Dean already home. He had got very little from the editor, who had been polite but firm about the news item. It was true as far as it went, he said, and it was the business of a newspaper to print the truth. Septimus reflected wryly that the interview might have taken a slightly different course had either the editor or the Dean known the full story of the activities of Mr Jones. However, he saw no reason to cause trouble for a resourceful young man, so he kept his own counsel.

'All he would do,' said the Dean, 'was to promise to let me know before he publishes anything else. Oh! And – by the way – who was the horse-thief, Septimus?'

'Just the reporter who wrote the article,' Septimus said.

'And how did you know that?'

'That,' said Septimus, 'would be telling.'

Now the Dean knew that he was spending his nights in the Minster, Septimus gladly accepted his offer of the Deanery as a base. It was inconvenient going back each day to Danedyke, and he could get Mary Crowle to look after Grace. He declined the Dean's invitation to lunch. He wanted to get some fresh air and solitude and to think out the various leads he had got.

'You have some leads then?' the Dean asked.

'More leads than you'd find in a pet shop. Tangle would be a better word,' Septimus replied.

Alisdair, who had been lurking wistfully in the hall, was dispatched by his father to Mrs Wedge in the kitchen with a request for a packed lunch for Septimus. While they were waiting for it to arrive the Dean produced the list for which Septimus had asked. Septimus slipped the two sheets of typed quarto into his pocket. Alisdair returned with the sandwiches.

'Can I come with you?' he asked.

Septimus looked down. The boy's eyes were shining with hope and it went to his heart to refuse. But he must have solitude.

'No, you can't come, Watson,' he said, 'because I've got a job for you to do.'

He took a key out of his pocket. 'This is the key to the door under the organ. That's where I've been lurking while I've been playing Sherlock. You'll find my document case in there. Get it, Watson, and bring it down to the car park, and I'll show you what I want you to do.'

Alisdair shot out of the front door. Septimus took his leave of the Dean and walked in leisurely fashion through the Peterport and down Chandlers Way, enjoying the August sunshine. He was sitting in the landrover when, five minutes later, Alisdair climbed into the passenger seat beside him. Septimus extracted the manuscript music of Primrose's 'Suite for Janet' from his document case, and opened the brittle pages, resting them on the steering wheel. He pointed to the pencilled notes.

'Alisdair, do you remember what Berwick said about these?'

'Yes,' Alisdair replied. 'They're the sort of notes a musician would write. Any fool can see that.'

'Well, I'm a very special sort of fool; they're initialled S.T. like me, and I want to know who the musician was. According to Berwick they were written before the organ was over-hauled in 1935. And . . .' Septimus realized a further point which made him feel just like Sherlock Holmes, 'And they were written with a propelling pencil.'

'How do you know that?'

Septimus grinned at the awe in Alisdair's voice.

'Elementary, my dear Watson. As a matter of fact, I've only just noticed.' He pointed to the pencil underlinings. 'Look. The lead broke there. But it starts again here. Same thickness, only scratchy.'

'Coo!' said Alisdair. 'Are you going to write a monograph on sixty-four different kinds of pencil lead?'

Septimus laughed.

'No. But I do own a propelling pencil. Anyway, that does help a bit because I don't suppose there were propelling pencils much before about 1900.'

'So I'm looking for a musician connected with the Minster – Master of Music, precentor, minor canon – initials S.T., between about 1900 and 1935?'

'That's it, Watson.'

'O.K., Holmes. And as your medical adviser, I suggest you leave the gin in the coal scuttle. It's bad for the mental processes.'

When he got back to Danedyke Septimus dealt with his post and then took a frantically pleased Great Dane across to the village school. Mary Crowle was moderately pleased to see him, inclined to be cross about the disruption Grace caused in the schoolroom, amenable to the idea that she should take over temporary care of the dog, and was finally persuaded to lend him the school tape recorder. This last was particularly good of her, since Septimus was thoroughly evasive as to what he wanted it for.

Septimus, having concluded his business in the school, spent a blissful few minutes inspecting a model of Saint Mary's made from egg boxes and detergent containers, and then drove out to the Danedyke Garage where he borrowed a large reel of cable from Tom Barton who was one of his churchwardens. After leaving the garage he turned down the rutted lane to the Home Farm, waving to Mrs Jackson as he drove past the farm-house. Beyond the house there was a gated road leading straight as a ruled line through five fields down to the sea. Septimus followed it, and at last drove the landrover on to a spit of hard shingle where the marram grass finally gave up the struggle. He switched off the engine. Immediately he was drowned fathoms deep in solitude. There was no human being in sight. Indeed, there was probably no human being nearer than the Home Farm two miles away, for the straight track over the fields was the only approach to this corner of the Wash, and it was not possible to walk round the shore because of the inlets and the treacherous sand banks and mud flats. The sea was calm, wrinkled like glass that has been melted, stained and blotched with shallows and sand banks, veined with grey channels of deep water. It stretched as far as the eye could see to the east and the north and the south, and where the water ended the grey and yellow dunes marched away, their only vegetation the whispering marram grass. The only sounds were the lament of the wind over the open spaces, the hush and murmur of the sea, and the lonely crying of countless sea birds.

It was hot. Septimus stripped and bathed in one of the deep channels, then lay on his towel until he was dry. Then he dressed, putting on old slacks and an open-necked shirt of piratical colouring. He got his document case from the land-rover and made himself comfortable, his back in a hollow of the dunes. First he looked at the manuscript of the 'Suite for Janet,' puzzling over the pencilled notes. But they told him nothing. He was no musician, and he could only hope that Alisdair Cameron would find out who 'S.T.' was. Not that he could see how that would help in a case that was such a ludicrous tangle. He put the music away and sat frowning at the sea. He was still no nearer answering the two critical questions 'how?' and 'why?' Well, he corrected himself, perhaps a little nearer. He had eliminated John Jones. He was suspicious of the Archdeacon. There was the queer story about Ted Barnes and Ma Wenlock's séances at the Jolly Waggoner. And at least he knew that the control panel for the Minster public address system was not used for the organ music. But were the speakers used? If so, there must be an amplifier and a control system somewhere. But where? A secret room? But that would mean rewiring the whole Minster, and anyway, he did not believe in secret rooms. A secret system would be almost as complicated as the official one and how on earth could anybody put it in? And why go to the trouble and expense? The trouble with this case was that it simply had no motive. He could understand people laying out large sums of money for a cash return, but in this case no one appeared to be in the position of making anything out of it. The whole thing was clearly ridiculous. There was no reason for doing it, and it could not be done. Yet it was being done, so there must be a reason. Realizing that he was embarked on a circular argument he gave it up, making a mental note to have a good look at the wiring of one of the speakers.

He turned his mind to 'why?', to the question of motive. He got out a pencil and made a list in the back of his diary.

Money
Madness
Practical Jokery
Someone who wanted to prove that a ghost existed
Someone who wanted to make the cathedral notorious

He considered the five motives carefully.

Money. A notorious haunting would attract tourists. That would mean more money in the offertory boxes. Perhaps the culprit was the Dean who was trying to raise fifty thousand pounds for the nave roof. Septimus snorted and put aside the money motive.

Madness. Well, that got him nowhere. Half the Chapter were mad anyway, and if you were investigating lunacy you needed a psychiatrist, not a copper.

A practical joker. That was no better than madness. How did you decide that any particular citizen was lunatic enough to play the sort of elaborate practical joke that was going on? But if it was a practical joker, it must be someone who knew the Minster well. You could not just breeze in from Birmingham on a day trip and start rewiring the Minster for sound. At least not unless you did it under cover. A TV broadcast, or a *Son et Lumiè* or somesuch. He made a mental note to investigate this. What about practical jokers among those who knew the Minster well? He reviewed those whom he knew, conscious as he did so of the vast mass whom he did not know. He wrote down Harry Tulloch, Ted Barnes, Canon Payne, Berwick and a man called Bert Smith who was the Minster electrician. He scowled at the list. They all had humour enough to play a practical joke, but there must be five times as many people whom he did not know with as much humour and as much opportunity. But at least the Dean did not figure in this list, nor did the Archdeacon. The Dean's humour was far too academic for messing around with loudspeakers, and so far as Septimus had been able to discover, the Archdeacon had no sense of humour at all. Still, Bert Smith the electrician would bear investigating.

Someone who wanted to prove that a ghost existed? The Archdeacon was the obvious choice here. Second, there was Alisdair Cameron.

Finally, someone who wanted to make the cathedral notorious. Well obviously under this heading the most likely person was a journalist, and the most likely journalist John Jones. But Septimus knew that he could be written off. No doubt the press were interested, but they had not started the business. For the rest there was the Dean for financial reasons, and indeed, almost anyone who loved the Minster and who was crackers enough to want to make it famous in such a dubious way.

Septimus scowled angrily at his handiwork, knowing it to be totally useless. He put it away and got out the Dean's list of the cathedral staff. Most of them appeared to have been there nearly as long as the building itself. The bottom of the list ran like this:

The Very Rev Charles Cameron	....	5 years
Mr H. A. Berwick	....	3½ years
Canon Payne	....	2 years
Mr A. N. Smith (Electrician)	....	1½ years
The Ven A. Jenkins	....	6 months

Well, at least the last five names figured on his previous list, and he had not realized that the Archdeacon had been on the staff for such a short time. That was something to bear in mind – especially as the Archdeacon was an expert on tape recorders and believed in ghosts. Septimus suddenly grinned at the North Sea, thinking of the Venerable Aloysius crawling round the clerestory on his hands and knees rewiring the public address system. An accomplice then? What about Bert Smith the electrician? Or Ted Barnes? At least he knew about short-wave radios, even if he had no cause to love the Archdeacon. Or a paid helper – an electrician hired in the town? But then you came back to the question 'how?' What he really needed was to do a minute inspection of the whole fabric. The sort of job that forensic would do on a suspect car. Go over it with chemicals and microscopes and all the rest of the scientific paraphernalia. But how did you go about that in a dirty great Minster, without spending ten thousand pounds on scaffolding before you even started? You couldn't get up to the speakers on the pillars without a special ladder that needed five men to handle it. And the Minster did not even own one of those. They hired it from the local Electricity Board. Still ... you didn't absolutely have to have a ladder if you wanted to get up a pillar –

provided the Dean did not know, and no one was looking.

Septimus suddenly shivered and sat up. The sun had gone from the sea and all was grey and drab. He looked at his watch and was disbelieving about what it told him. It was nearly seven o'clock.

On his way back to Minster Saint Peter he called once again at the Rectory in Danedyke. He found what he was looking for in a trunk in the attic. He had not seen it for years. It was something from his remote past, from the War years when government and circumstances had forced him to be both athletic and energetic in dangerous places. It was a two hundred foot length of cable-laid climbing rope.

9 Suite for Janet

Alisdair Cameron only ran half-way up Chandlers Way when he left Septimus. By the Archdeacon's front gate he slowed to a walk, his mind full of ways of establishing the identity of S.T. There was a cupboard full of old music programmes in the Song School. There was Mr Berwick. There was old Canon Harrison, ninety-three and retired, but still living in Cloister Garth. He knew all there was to know about the Minster music over the last half century. But first and obviously there was the list of organists on the oak board screwed to the organ casing.

With a pleasant tingle of adventure to come, Alisdair plunged from the hot sunlight into the cool of the nave. He was really helping a real detective – albeit a retired one – carry out an investigation.

He reached the organ and glanced down the names on the board, and the investigation collapsed in anti-climax.

1929–1937 Simeon Truswell

That was all there was to it. Septimus could hardly be out of the cark park and already the investigation was concluded. He had no excuse for turning out the cupboard in the Song School, or for cross-questioning Berwick or Canon Harrison. He thrust his hands into his jeans pockets and wandered disconsolately westward. There was a rope stretched between the Dean's and the Chancellor's stalls at the top of the chancel steps. Its purpose was to prevent visitors walking over the brasses in the floor of the choir. Alisdair slipped the rope with its brass ring from the hook fixed to his father's stall – and stopped dead. The action had reminded him of something. He had actually met Simeon Truswell, here, at this particular spot in the Minster. It had been nearly five years ago, just after they had come to Minster Saint Peter. Simeon Truswell had been coming out of the choir – a round little man, as bald as a bladder, his old face seamed with wrinkles like an elderly, under-inflated football. He had smiled at Alisdair, and Alisdair – self-conscious and proud – had said he was the new Dean's son. So they had talked. Alisdair replaced the brass ring and went to look at another plaque on the organ, this time a brass plate. 'To the Glory of God,' it read, 'this organ was rebuilt A.D. 1935. Simeon Truswell, Master of Music. James Allardyce, Dean.' The old man had showed him that plate. And he had said something else. Something about a recording.

Alisdair ran between the choir stalls and jumped the rope, oblivious of the stares of the startled visitors. He ran to the bookstall in the south transept where a tall thin woman was on duty.

'Miss Adams,' he said. 'Let me borrow one of your histories a minute, can I? I want to look something up.'

'Help yourself, Alisdair,' she said. 'Only don't get it dirty, there's a dear.'

He took the booklet and sat on the bottom chancel step, heedless of the visitors – a thin boy with fair hair, wearing a grubby singlet and jeans.

He turned to the last chapter, 'The Minster and the Arts'. There was a list of musical occasions since the beginning of the century. Yes! Here it was 'August 1934. Recording of choir and organ. The first recording ever made in the Minster, and the only record in existence of the sound of the organ before the 1935 rebuild.' Alisdair sat with the history open and unheeded on his lap. A record. A record of the old organ. Berwick had said that the mysterious music sounded like the old organ ... There must be a copy of it somewhere. But where? He returned the history to Miss Adams and went to the Song School. The long benches were deserted, covered with a litter of music and battered books, the walls were lined with cupboards. In the bottom of the third cupboard he found a pile of old records. Organ music, recordings of the choir, an old '78' of 'Tiger Rag', more recordings of the choir – he had no idea there would be so many of them. But what he was looking for was not there. He returned to the Deanery and went through the record cabinet in the drawing-room. Then he remembered seeing a pile of old records in the attic, and shot up the stairs.

They were an interesting collection, part of the bric-à-brac that was handed on from Dean to Dean. They were also very dusty, and Alisdair transferred a good deal of the dust to himself in turning them over. Once again he drew a blank. Disappointed and a little at a loss, he went and sat astride his old rocking horse, considering what to do next. The rocking horse squeaked from long disuse, and the motes of dust danced in the sunlight filtering through the grimy windows.

Of course! Canon Harrison.

As he thundered down the front stairs Mrs Wedge came out of the kitchen.

'Lunch in five minutes, Alisdair. Your father's out ... Good Lord, boy! You're filthy!'

'Only be five minutes, Mrs Wedge.' He slammed the front door and ran full tilt across the grass of Cloister Garth to Canon Harrison's little house snug in the corner behind its yew hedge.

The old man was like a talkative tortoise, slow and friendly, and it was not five minutes but a full half hour before Alisdair came triumphantly back across Cloister Garth carrying the precious record like a tray for the head of John the Baptist.

It was fortunate that his father was out for lunch. The Dean, a mild man in most things, was a stickler for courtesy and punctuality about meals, and it was a great deal easier to have only Mrs Wedge to cope with. But that was bad enough because she was very angry and – as Alisdair fully recognized – quite justly. He apologized as handsomely as he could, and by the time he had washed she had calmed down like a pot taken off the stove and withdrew her threat to tell his father. So he gobbled his lunch, and further to cement the frail peace, he helped Mrs Wedge with the washing-up. Then at last he was able to carry his treasure into the drawing-room.

Canon Harrison's memory had failed him as to what was on the record, and the label was no help. It told you what the choir sang, and for the rest it simply said, 'Organ music'.

He set the record player to '78' and started side one. There were two short anthems, separated by an organ piece which Alisdair could not identify, but which was obviously designed to show the range of the instrument. Side one ended with a piece of Bach.

Alisdair was struck by two things – how different the old organ sounded from the new, and how good the recording seemed considering how long ago it had been made. But then of course, unlike most old recordings he had ever heard, this one had probably not been played more than two or three times. He turned the disc over, his hand quivering with nervousness now. There was only one organ piece on this side, and if that was not what he was hoping for, then all his plans for surprising Septimus with a really useful clue would burst like a bubble.

Side two started with the choir singing an extract from the Saint Matthew Passion, and then – there it was! The music which had so frightened him on that first night. The music that Berwick had played on the modern instrument, and which had been written for the old instrument. Here it was, actually as it had sounded on the old instrument. Hezekiah Primrose's 'Suite for Janet', with its gay trumpet tones and its pealing, triumphant conclusion.

He played it through twice for the sheer triumph of discovery, then he carefully set the needle on the blank space leading into it and switched off. He looked at the clock on the mantelpiece. It would be several hours before Dr Watson could share his triumph with Sherlock Holmes.

Septimus drove straight up Chandlers Way, through the Peterport and down to the south door of the Minster. He unlocked the door, put the tape recorder, the rope and his other gear inside the cloister, and then drove back down to the car park. After leaving the landrover he walked slowly up the hill, enjoying the evening sun. It was low in the west, throwing black shadows of buttress and decoration along the north wall of the Minster, which ran in one sweep from the great west end to the Cottages, interrupted only by the Petersteps sloping steeply down into the market-place. There were three rows of windows. The bottom row, small, round-headed arches which gave minimal light to the crypt, were more like archery slits than windows. Above them marched the great gothic windows of the nave, and above them again, the delicate tracery of the clerestory. As Septimus walked up the hill the sun glowed rose on the whitewashed end of the Cottages, and he realized afresh what a peculiar shape the Minster was. Because of its site on the rock overlooking the harbour it was shaped like a cross with one arm missing. There was no transept on the north side. That was why the Tudor cottages fitted so well with the much older Minster. They helped to restore symmetry.

As Septimus reached the Cottages the door of number 3 opened and Norman Barnes came down the steps, dressed for his motor cycle and carrying a pack. Ted stood on the doorstep seeing his son off.

'Evening, Norman,' said Septimus. 'Off on a spree?'

'Work,' replied Norman.

'I didn't know the Post Office worked nights.'

'Not half,' said Norman non-committally. He said good night to his father and to Septimus and went down the hill.

'Sorters and engineers and such,' said Ted. 'They have to work nights. Norman, he's got digs in Cambridge, but he likes to get home when he can. Good lad is Norman.' He watched his son until he turned into the car park. 'Cup of tea, Mr Treloar? I'm waiting for that vet in Tokyo.'

He led the way to the little workshop with its one window looking out on Harry Tulloch's back door.

As Septimus drank tea he inspected the workshop closely, his keen eyes hooded by the heavy lids. There seemed to be nothing suspicious, no obvious amplifiers, no complex tape recorders. Just the big short-wave set and a clutter of headphones, tools and pieces of wire.

Ted slipped on the headphones, leaving one ear free for Septimus.

'So you're sleeping in the Minster, Mr Treloar?'

'Who told you that?' Septimus asked.

Ted looked surprised. 'Well, the Archdeacon, he mentioned it. But I'd guessed anyway. You being around so much in the evenings, and having been a detective and all that.'

So much for security in a cathedral town, thought Septimus. You would have to be the invisible man to keep anything really secret.

'I'd be obliged if you'd keep quiet about it, Ted,' he said. 'The fewer people who know about it the better.'

'Mum's the word, sir.'

'Ted, I didn't know you'd been a parishioner of the Archdeacon's when he was at the Salwarpes.'

'That's right, sir. I had a smallholding in Salwarpe Saint Anthony. You been talking to the Archdeacon?'

'No. Ma Wenlock was telling me.'

Ted frowned. 'I wish she wouldn't. Can't keep her mouth shut, that one. Not that I mind you knowing sir. But it's all – well – a bit private. A chap don't want all his personal affairs discussed in the public bar.'

'Sorry, Ted. I didn't mean to pry. How do you get on with the Archdeacon now?'

'Oh, all right. We buried the hatchet years ago. He's all right, the Archdeacon. Bit rigid like, and not the sort of chap you can get exactly fond of. But at least you know where you are with him. He was quite right about old Ma Wenlock. She was as crooked as a corkscrew. It's a funny thing, sir. A chap don't really know himself. You can think you're set in your ways. Then something terrible happens – like your wife dying. Then – pouf! – it all goes. You're not married, Mr Treloar?'

Septimus shook his head and as he did so the headphones squawked.

'Excuse me, sir. That's my mate in Tokyo. Can you see yourself out?'

Septimus walked on up Chandlers Way thinking about Ted and his relationship with the Archdeacon, and what Sophia Wenlock had told him. He would have liked to ask Ted about that last séance. What was it Ma Wenlock had said? 'I told Eddie things only his Mary could have known.' And the Archdeacon had learned, when the damage was done, that he had been at least partly mistaken. Somewhere, buried in all that tangle, there was the thin end of a motive, only he could not begin to extract it because he had no idea what it was.

Someone grabbed his arm.

'Holmes. I've something for you. Come in.' It was Alisdair Cameron. He allowed himself to be led into the Deanery, half his mind still grappling with the Archdeacon and Ted Barnes. Quivering with excitement, Alisdair took him to the drawing-room, telling him nothing. He made Septimus sit down, switched on the record player, and started the turntable. There was a scratchy silence and then, as the 'Suite for Janet' pealed out, Septimus forgot the Archdeacon and Ted and came very suddenly and firmly into the present. Alisdair sat on the sofa hugging his knees. With enormous glee he watched the effect of his detecting.

19   Well and Truly Clobbered

Septimus shut the door behind him and struggled down the twilit cloister carrying all his paraphernalia. He hardly noticed its weight, so excited was he by Alisdair's discovery. It was the first real glimmer of light on the question 'how?' Of course it left a great many questions still unanswered. A recording of Primrose's suite played on the old organ was one thing. How the Minster could be filled with its sound was altogether another. But still it was an enormous step forward, almost the first piece of firm evidence that had emerged in this morass of a case.

The nave was quiet and filled with the many-coloured splendour of the west window. He dumped most of his equipment outside the door to his hidey-hole under the organ and went up the steps carrying the length of cable, the microphone belonging to the tape recorder and his coil of climbing rope. Once in the clerestory he went to the pillar immediately west of the organ and leaned over the balustrade. It was a dizzy drop into the nave where the pews looked like little boxes laid on a draughtsboard. The long grey rectangle of the loudspeaker was below him, some six feet to his right and facing out into the nave. It was a daunting prospect, for Septimus had not done any serious climbing for years. But there was a wide band of decoration running round the capital of the pillar, and the shaft of the pillar itself was covered with a zig-zag of Norman decoration. He reckoned he could just about do it, and with the rope in case of catastrophe he would injure nothing but his pride.

First he attached the microphone to the end of the cable he had borrowed from Tom Barton. Then he lowered the microphone over the balustrade and left it dangling as close to the speaker as he could get it, and level with its bottom edge. Next he took a turn of the rope round the balustrade and belayed the end round one of the window stanchions. He secured the rope round his waist and sat astride the balustrade.

'Here goes,' he said, commending himself mentally into the hands of God. Viewed by strict rock standards it was not a difficult climb. There were plenty of good handholds on the pillar. But Septimus was stiff and out of practice and his fingers had lost the iron strength they had once possessed. There was one hair-raising moment when he misjudged a foothold and found himself swinging free above the long drop into the nave, supported only by his finger tips which were precariously crooked over a moulding. But at last he arrived and was able to plant his feet firmly on the band of decoration just below the speaker. His hands were shaking, and his face streaming with sweat.

He rested a moment, getting his breath back, his fingers gripping the zig-zag, his face pressed against the stone, his back to the sheer drop. Then cautiously he let go with one hand and slid a pencil torch out of his pocket. He shuffled six inches along the narrow ledge and by the light of the torch examined the back of the speaker. There was only one cable coming out of it. Next, he changed his grip and reached out with his right hand for the flex of the dangling microphone. He had some difficulty hauling it in with only one hand, and even more difficulty fixing the flex so that the microphone hung in front of the speaker. But at last he managed both tasks. So he rested again and then started the climb back to the clerestory. It was not so difficult as coming down, but it was difficult enough, and he was trembling with weariness when at last he rolled thankfully over the balustrade and sat on the floor of the clerestory to recover.

'Phew,' he muttered, mopping his forehead. 'You're too old for that lark, Septimus.' He untied and coiled his rope, then he ran out the cable, taping it inconspicuously under the balustrade. When he reached the organ he paused. He had been intending to run the cable down the stairs. But the organ was built right up to, and underneath the walkway. It might be possible to drop the cable straight down into his hidey-hole.

Immediately to his right there was a row of big pipes, cutting off the view into the nave. At one end of them there was a sizeable hole, almost as if a pipe had been removed and never replaced. Down this hole, through a forest of pipes and cables, he could see the single electric bulb of his hidey-hole. He cut off enough cable from the drum and dropped the end down the hole. He wriggled it about a bit, and then heard the end thump on boards.

When he got to the little room under the organ, the single bulb seemed very bright. Septimus bared the end of his length of flex, fixed a terminal to it, and plugged it into the microphone socket of the tape recorder.

'Now then, Hezekiah,' he said. 'Start playing tonight, and we shall be able to tell whether you're the original electronic ghost.'

When he had set up the tape recorder he sat on his haunches, thinking. He had better test it. After all, Mary Crowle's microphone might be unserviceable. So he started the recorder and went out to the controls of the public address system. He switched on, turned up the volume, and selected the microphone on the Dean's stall. He went across the choir in the gathering darkness and stood in front of the microphone.

'Here beginneth the first lesson,' he said loudly.

'Here beginneth the first lesson . . . the first lesson . . . first lesson . . . lesson.' The sounds went bellowing and echoing round the quiet Minster, growing louder, higher and faster as they went. Septimus knew enough to realize that he had set the volume too high and he was getting what is called 'howl round'. It would go on getting louder and higher until something burst. Already the words were lost in a rising shriek. He ran for the controls and hastily turned everything off. Silence descended like the fall of a curtain. He could only hope he had done no damage.

The tape recorder worked satisfactorily. When he switched it on he heard a horribly distorted metallic voice say, 'Here beginneth the first lesson.' It sounded as if he was speaking through a Jew's harp. Satisfied, he ran the tape back to the beginning and left the recorder ready for use.

He stood up and stretched. Now that all was ready for the night, he suddenly realized that he was hungry – very hungry indeed. Mrs Wedge's sandwiches were still in his pack, and as far as he could remember all he had had during the day was two cups of coffee. He took out the sandwiches and a can of beer, and ate and drank, enjoying himself immensely. After a while he got his torch and, sandwich in hand, went to investigate the space down which he had dropped the cable for the tape recorder.

At the back of the little room, immediately under the clerestory walkway there was a bank of big pipes. They faced outward, so that their sound would go into the Minster. The space was at the end. It was almost as if a pipe was missing. The pipes were held in position by boarding which reached about three feet up from the floor, making a low wooden wall. Septimus peered over the edge and shone his torch down into the gap, expecting to see the floor three feet down. But there was no floor. There was a hole and blackness, and his torch was shining on grey stone many feet below. He waggled the torch beam and saw cables and an electric motor. Then he remembered Ted Barnes saying that half the organ was in the crypt, and suddenly realized the vast size of an instrument which was not built on the nave floor at all, but really stretched from crypt to clerestory. Intrigued, he got the key to the crypt from Harry Tulloch's cubby-hole and opened the door by the Chapter library. A cold wind blew in his face as he went down a circular stairway not unlike the one that led up to the Lantern.

It was dark in the crypt, but he would not turn on the lights for fear of them being seen in the town, and thereby adding to the ghost story.

Being in the crypt was like being in a stone forest. Septimus shone his torch around this, by far the most ancient part of the Minster. They had been here – these pillars, these arches – when the Viking longboats came out of the mists of the North Sea and laid waste the coast. The ceiling was very low, and the squat pillars were of great thickness. They stood less than ten feet apart in every direction, and they were connected to one another by plain, round-headed arches. Pillars, shadows, arches flicked and crossed one another as Septimus swung the torch round. Squat stone trees, petrified for over a thousand years to hold up the unimaginable weight of the great Minster above. Torch in hand he moved northward down a long grove of pillars, their shadows pointing into the blackness, until at last he found himself facing a wooden wall of groove and tongue planking with three doors in it. The one to his left was locked. The middle one was a store, full of ecclesiastical junk. The third one led into the bottom organ room. It was much like his hidey-hole in the nave above except that there were no organ pipes, only a mass of cables and ducting going in all directions. In the middle there were three large rectangular structures which proved to be bellows for supplying air to the organ. Against one wall there was a large electric motor. Septimus shone his torch up, inspecting the underside of the row of big pipes. There was an air duct running from the bottom of each pipe. The gap at the end appeared as a black rectangle. Perhaps it had once contained a pipe which had been removed. More likely the space was necessary for getting the other pipes in and out. After all, they did stretch from the floor of the nave up to the clerestory.

He stood gazing up at the black rectangle, pondering possibilities, when high above him he saw a gleam of light. He switched off his torch. The darkness in the little room was like black velvet. The gleam came again, and this time it sent a vertical arrow of fire down the side of the end pipe. There was someone with a torch or a lantern in the clerestory.

Septimus turned and groped his way to the door, closing it softly behind him. He switched on his torch and ran silently down the grove of stone trees to the steps leading up into the nave. At the top he opened the door cautiously, slipped through, and stood in the deep shadow of the arch.

The sun had gone now and the windows were pale against the evening, clearly visible, but giving little light. Leaving the door ajar, Septimus flitted across to the bookstall, crouched, and then peered carefully out from his cover. From this position, just to the south of the chancel steps, he could see the whole sweep of the clerestory on the north side, from the battlements of the organ to the window at the west end. Behind the organ there was a glimmer of light. For a moment the pipes and the gilded angels that crowned the casing stood out in silhouette. Then the light went out and all was dark again.

For some time nothing happened and Septimus waited with the patience of the stone statue beside which he was standing. And then, at last, a dark figure moved swiftly across the clerestory window nearest to the organ. It disappeared into the first tunnel, and there it stopped, apparently doing something, or looking at something. For perhaps a minute and a half Septimus could see the tunnel mouth outlined by the glow of the torch. Then the intruder came out again, walked quickly across the second window, and paused for the same length of time in the second tunnel. Evidently whoever it was was working westward performing the same task in each of the tunnels.

Septimus considered for a moment. With the memory of his fracas with John Jones fresh in his mind, he was determined that this time there should be no mistakes.

He waited until the intruder was safely occupied in one of the tunnels and then ran on tiptoe across the Minster until he was safe from sight in the north aisle. He went through the door at the top of the Petersteps, across the planking which now covered Hezekiah Primrose's grave, and so up the circular staircase. He inched open the door at the top and peeped round the edge. Three tunnels down the walkway he could see the torch lying on the floor. Beside the torch a dark figure was kneeling, doing something on the surface of the wall, long fingers white in the torchlight.

As Septimus watched, the unknown task was completed and the man moved forward to the next tunnel, turning off the torch as he crossed the open space in front of the window. Once again the torch flicked on, was placed on the floor, and the man knelt beside it.

With his back pressed against the stone Septimus slid from the doorway on to the clerestory itself. Moving crabwise he crossed the window and took up his position in the corner, just by the arched exit from the nearest tunnel, his right shoulder to the window, his left pressed against the moulding of the tunnel arch. So he waited, tense for action as he had been so many times in the long past.

He heard cautious footsteps as the intruder came into the final tunnel and stopped a bare four feet away. He saw the beam of the torch stab out scarcely six inches from his toes. He heard the rustle as the man knelt and started his mysterious work. And then he heard a slight grunt as the man stood up, picking up the torch, making its beam jerk suddenly.

As the torch was switched off, so Septimus raised his left hand, the fingers extended, ready for the karate chop. He was aware that it was – perhaps – a little extreme, but the humiliation of his struggle with John Jones was still bitter in his memory, and he was taking no chances of a fight here in the high clerestory with its low balustrade and long drop to the floor. He heard footsteps coming softly over the flags. Then the dark figure came out of the tunnel and Septimus struck.

The blow was perfectly timed and, with a hiss of breath, the intruder collapsed on to his knees, fell forward slowly on to his face and lay still. Septimus switched on his own torch, knelt down and rolled the unconscious figure over.

It was the Archdeacon.

11   A Lantern in the Dark

'Well! Well!' murmured Septimus. 'We do see life. That's the very first time I've ever clobbered an Archdeacon.' He considered what to do. He did not much fancy trying to carry the unconscious cleric down the stone steps. He *could* go and get a bucket of water – he would quite enjoy pouring it over the Venerable Aloysius. But then by the time he got back with the water the Archdeacon would probably have recovered consciousness anyway – that is, if the blow had been accurately calculated.

He decided to give it a few minutes and see. He rolled the Archdeacon on to his back, undid his clerical collar and made him as comfortable as possible. He then went to investigate what the Archdeacon had been working at in the tunnels. It did not take him long. In the centre of the tunnel a thin thread was stretched from wall to wall across the way. It was about eighteen inches from the ground. Septimus stepped carefully over the thread and continued down the clerestory. As he expected, he found a similar thread in each of the tunnels. So the Archdeacon was trying to establish whether or not anyone walked along the clerestory. And what did that prove about the Archdeacon? Septimus sat on the balustrade puzzling over the question. He could make little sense of it and was soon recalled from his speculations by a loud groan. When he got back, the Archdeacon was sitting up rubbing the side of his neck.

'Good evening, Archdeacon,' said Septimus as if there was

nothing unusual in finding a senior cleric sitting on the cold flags of the clerestory late at night, with his clerical collar hanging at his waist.

'Who's that? Ah Treloar. I'm glad to see you. Treloar, I've been attacked. Knocked unconscious. Someone leapt out of the dark and struck me down.'

'Yes,' said Septimus, 'I did.'

'You! How dare you?'

It should have been a furious thunderbolt from the wrathful hand of Jove, but it came out as a pathetic squeak.

'I'm sorry, Archdeacon. But it really is a bit unwise to wander round the place unannounced when the Dean has hired an ex-copper as guard dog. I thought you were a villain – or at least a reporter.'

'Help me up,' said the Archdeacon.

Septimus stretched out a hefty arm and yanked the Archdeacon to his feet. As he came upright the Archdeacon had to give up the attempt to be angry. He really did not feel fit enough, and he was uncomfortably aware of his clerical collar at his midriff.

'I came to look for you first, Treloar,' he said, 'but I could not find you.'

Septimus was on the point of saying where he had been, but changed his mind at the last moment. 'I was having a look round,' he said and – to change the subject – 'are you feeling fit enough to manage the stairs?'

Septimus helped him down the circular stairway and across the nave towards the south door. He steered the Archdeacon into a pew.

'You sit there,' he said. 'I'll get you a drink of water from Harry Tulloch's cubby-hole.' He walked into the transept, the beam of his torch swinging across tiles and pillars, splashing light across walls and doors. The light flicked across the crypt door and Septimus came to a sudden halt. The door

to the crypt was closed. He distinctly remembered leaving it
open when he had come up the steps from the crypt. He
went to the door and tried it. It was locked. Well – that was
what you would expect if it had blown shut – it was a yale
lock. He took the key from his pocket, opened the door and
peered down into the darkness, the dank, cold smell of the
crypt blowing in his face. Was there enough draught to
blow the door shut? He pushed it a foot open and left it,
watching by the light of his torch to see what would
happen. The door swung swiftly shut. It bounced back as if
the spring-loaded bolt was a buffer. But it did not latch. He
pushed the door open again and went quietly down into the
crypt. He stood at the bottom, not using his torch, gazing
into blackness. Above him the great nave was full of the small
noises of the night, a tapestry of tiny sounds which men call
quietness and peace. But here there was silence, nothing
but stone and the silence and darkness of the tomb. He stood
for a moment and then went back up to the nave closing the
door behind him with a loud click. He got water from the
tap in Harry Tulloch's cubby-hole and took it to the Archdeacon, using his torch so that the glass was visible. The
Archdeacon had retethered his clerical collar. He was pale,
but beginning to look much more his stern self. Suddenly he
stopped drinking. He took the tumbler from his lips and
pointed with his unoccupied hand.

'Look!' he said softly.

Septimus slewed round, the beam of the torch stabbing
across the shadows of the nave like a searchlight.

In the clerestory, just by the organ, there was a glow of
light. As they watched it grew brighter as if someone was
moving with a torch. No, not a torch. There was no beam.
Just a glow. It must be some sort of lantern.

The Archdeacon stood up. 'Come on!' he said.

'No. Wait a bit,' Septimus said, thrusting the other man

down into the pew again, his mind racing. The light was coming from behind the organ, moving *westward*. According to the tale of the haunting, if this was supposed to be John Jancey's lantern it was moving in the wrong direction. The light grew brighter. Now they could see the silhouette of the pipes and the triumphant angels. A moment later and they could see the lantern itself. It was being held just above the balustrade and as close to the organ as it could be. It was as if whoever held it did not wish to be seen, but wanted to look round the corner. It was lifted higher. Then it suddenly went out.

'Right,' said Septimus. 'Archdeacon, you lock the door at the top of the Petersteps and stay there.' Using the torch now he ran full tilt for the organ.

He pelted up the wooden steps, flashing the torch around. He shone it both ways down the clerestory, but there was nothing and no one to see. In the first tunnel the Archdeacon's thread was still in position. So if there was someone in the clerestory, they must have gone eastward, and by now the Archdeacon should have blocked the only other exit. He turned eastward and started a slow, methodical search of the clerestory, examining all the shadowy corners with his torch, taking particular care as he came out of the tunnels not to get caught as he himself had caught the Archdeacon.

He had reached the middle of the east window and was standing above the high altar when he heard the south door open. A shadowy figure came down the aisle and stood in the entrance to the choir.

'Mr Treloar. Mr Treloar, sir. Where are you?' Septimus could hear the anxiety in the voice. It was Ted Barnes.

'Here, Ted,' he called, 'I'm up here – over the high altar.' He signalled with his torch. Ted came to the altar rail. Septimus could see the ghostly oval of his face as he looked upward.

'Oh! Then it *was* you, sir.' There was relief in Ted's voice. 'I saw a light in the clerestory. Looked like a lantern to me. So I thought I'd better come in case you needed any help. But it must have been your torch.' Septimus was conscious of the terrible audibility of this calling through the darkness.

'No. It wasn't my torch. Ted, go across to the organ steps. I'll meet you there.'

In the darkness beneath the organ he explained what had happened, and while he was doing so the Archdeacon came down the north aisle.

'I heard voices,' he said. Septimus was drawing breath to reply when the organ started to play.

It was exactly as they had heard it before. Primrose's 'Suite for Janet,' triumphant, filling the nave, yet with more echo than the nave normally produced. And yet for all its gaiety there was something tentative about the music. Compared with the recording he had heard during the afternoon it was like something struggling to be born. Septimus surprised himself with the comparison. 'Primrose's Suite for Lazarus', he thought. Then he leapt into action.

'Archdeacon,' he shouted, 'get back to that door. Ted, go to the top of the steps and wait there.' It took him only a couple of seconds to dive into the organ room and switch on the recorder so that he was half-way up the organ steps before Ted had reached the top and before the Archdeacon had reached the end of the north aisle.

Septimus left Ted as sentinel at the top of the steps and started once again on his erratic progress round the clerestory. At last he came all the way round the building to the door leading to the Lantern stairs. There had been nothing. Not a sign of a human being. And during all his progress, triumphant, mocking, haunting, the 'Suite for Janet' filled the building. And still he could not tell where the music came from. He went on to the circular staircase, and even as he did so, the organ stopped. It was as if the unseen was watching him, playing with him. He locked the door behind him, slipped the key into his pocket. He went down the curving steps, exchanged a few words with the Archdeacon through the door, and then went back and on and upward to the Lantern itself. He looked in at the glaring white light. Not a mouse could hide in that pitiless glare. He closed the door, waited a few moments for his night vision to return, and then went down again to the clerestory. He went along the north side, completing the circuit of the Minster, stepping carefully over the Archdeacon's pieces of thread, and so came back to Ted Barnes who was sitting at the top of the organ steps, his back against the wall, his feet stretched across the walkway. Ted scrambled to his feet.

'Nothing,' said Septimus.

They went down to the organ room: Septimus ran the recorder back and set it to replay. He pressed the button, and they waited in silence. There was nothing. Nothing but the hum of the machine and the rustle of a loose end of tape as the spools turned.

'Well, I'm damned,' said Septimus in total astonishment.

'What's the matter?' asked Ted.

As the tape recorder whispered meaninglessly on, Septimus explained. The tape recorder had picked up no sound from the speaker.

'I don't get it,' said Ted, scratching his head, 'I was bloomin' certain those speakers were being used somehow. Perhaps there's something duff in your circuit, Mr Treloar.'

Another voice joined the conversation.

'You did not pick up the music on your machine? I thought you would not.' It was the Archdeacon. In his astonishment about the failure of the tape recorder Septimus had forgotten all about him.

'And no doubt my tell-tales in the clerestory are still in position? Yes. I thought they would be.' He seemed unusually pleased about something, despite his dishevelled clothing and his pale face.

Ted spoke. He sounded thoroughly irritated – much less deferential than he usually was with the Archdeacon.

'Well, if you know how it's done, Mr Jenkins, I expect Mr Treloar would like to hear. I'm mortal sure I would. I'd made certain in my own mind that someone was mucking with the public address. Ain't no other way it can be done. Not that I can see.'

'As to that, Barnes, I have my own ideas. And I shall divulge them in the proper quarters, when I am ready, and not before. Meantime Treloar, you may recall that I have been the subject of a savage assault this evening. I am now going to bed. I shall be obliged if you could make it convenient to call on me at eleven in the morning. I have something I wish to say to you. Good night to you both.' He walked away into the darkness down the aisle and they heard the door close behind him.

Ted chuckled. 'He's a cool one is the Archdeacon. What did he mean about an assault, sir? Who assaulted him?'

'I did,' said Septimus, and explained what had happened.

Ted laughed unsympathetically, slapping his thigh.

'Cor! You thumped Himmler? Knocked him cold? Wish I'd been there to see it.'

But Septimus was not in the mood to see the funny side of it. He felt he had been outmanoeuvred, and the knowledge had a bitter taste.

'Come on, Ted. Let's just test this equipment before we go to bed.'

They did, and there was nothing the matter with it. Ted's voice from the Dean's stall was faithfully recorded by the speaker on the pillar and Mary Crowle's microphone hanging in front of it.

'Never mind,' said Ted at last, 'you'll work it out eventually, sir. Or perhaps the Archdeacon'll tell you how it's done in the morning.'

'Gerroutofit,' said Septimus. 'I'm for my bed, and that's where you ought to be, Ted Barnes.' But despite what he said, he remained gazing through the darkness of the Minster long after Ted had gone home. He had been struck by a profoundly simple thought.

Next morning, Friday, Septimus paid a quick visit to Dane-dyke, reported briefly to the Dean on his return, and then went into the Minster in search of Mr Smith the electrician.

'Bert?' said Harry Tulloch who was busy with a feather duster on the alabaster saints over the high altar. 'You'll find him in his workshop, Major. Just go round the west end and keep going till you can't go no more. That's Bert's workshop.'

Septimus did as he was bidden, walking beneath the flying buttresses which were like great stone men leaning against the west end to stop it falling into the market-place. A narrow alley led down the north side, the Minster on the right, a ten-foot wall with a battlemented top on the left. Half-way down there was an arched tunnel where the alley went under the Petersteps. Beside the arch an iron ladder was fixed to the wall. Looking up Septimus could see that it led to the battlements and the roof over the Petersteps. No doubt Harry Tulloch and his minions used it for cleaning gutters and the like. The alley continued on the far side of the tunnel. The wall to the left was still blank, but to the right there were now the small windows of the crypt, their sills nearly level with the ground. The alley ended in a blank wall. The bottom was stone like the Minster, but above the stone there was colourwash and timbering. It was the bottom end of the Cottages in Chandlers Way. To Septimus's right there was a wooden door in a round-head arch, and with a little shock he realized that it had once been one of the crypt windows. Was there, after all, a third way into the Minster which nobody had thought to mention? He remembered how the crypt door which he had left open had mysteriously closed itself.

He pushed open the door and was faced by a wooden partition. Stone steps went down to the left with another door at the bottom. There was a crack of light under the door.

Bert Smith the electrician was sitting at a bench against the wooden wall, the pieces of an electric fire scattered in front of him. The end wall was covered with a great many fuse boxes and switches. Between the bench and the fuses was another door which Septimus realized must lead into the crypt – the locked one of the three that he had investigated in the night.

Bert was a big man – nearly as big as Septimus but unlike Septimus, he was running to fat, and bald where Septimus was grey.

He stood up. 'Hullo, Mr Treloar. Thought you'd be seeking me out before long.'

'Why did you think that?' asked Septimus.

The fat man grinned. 'Well now. Let me see. You might be wanting me to lay an egg. But that's not in nature. Then again, you might be wanting an electrified ghost trap. That's more in my line. But I'd give it as my opinion that you'd really be interested in the Public Address.' He made it sound like a person.

'You look after it, I suppose?' said Septimus.

'I'm her nurse, as you might say,' Bert agreed, 'and she needs some nursing, she does. Nearly broadcast Radio One in the middle of the Dean's Easter Sermon, she did. But that was before I took her in hand.'

'You nursed her back to health?' Septimus asked.

'Well, nursed is hardly the right word. Operation's more like it. We had to do a major job on her, we did.'

'We?' said Septimus. 'Who helped you, Bert?'

'Ah well. It was like this. She was failing – on her last legs as you might say. And the Archdeacon, he was coming. And the fire people, they looked at the wiring and said, "Not on your Nellie". So the house had to be rewired before he could move in. So I saw Harry Tulloch and I told him. "Harry," I said. "If you want the Bishop sounding like a corncrake in the middle of matins, and the Archdeacon going up like a Roman candle, you're going the right way about it." Told him straight, I did. So the long and short of it was that Harry went to the Dean and they gave me a chap from Chambers in the town. Young fellow. Name of Peterson. Paddy Peterson. And he helped with the Public Address; and Ted Barnes, he helped with the Archdeacon. Only as often as not it was the other way round. So we got 'em fixed up between us, all neat and tidy.'

'I see,' said Septimus. 'Bert. Did you know the Archdeacon before he came to the Minster?'

'Not as you might say "Know" him. Wouldn't want to either, come to that. Not but what he doesn't put a fair bit of work in my way. Now take this fire. The Archdeacon's, this is. He *will* toast on it, see? I keep telling him the bread shorts the electrics. But he won't listen.'

'Do you look after his tape recorders?'

'Now isn't he a one for tape, the Archdeacon? Miles and miles of it. Yes. I look after 'em – and do a bit of electronic inventing for him, come to that.'

'Like that slow-running portable?' Septimus asked.

'Ah. I was right proud of him. Tricky little devil he was. Gave me more than one sleepless night. Still, I managed him in the end. Run for nigh on six hours, he will.'

'What does the Archdeacon record?' It was not strictly part of the investigation, but Septimus was curious.

'Almost anything. Omnivorous, he is. Music. Bells and organs. Very hot on organs is the Archdeacon. Birds as well. You ought to see him in his birding gear. Looks like he's escaped from *Charley's Aunt*. And of course – ghosts. When he can find 'em.'

Septimus wandered across the workshop to the great bank of fuses and switches. Bert followed him.

'That's the Minster,' he said. 'Control the lot, they do. I sometimes come in here for a quiet smoke in the middle of evensong. Them all singing away up above. And I think to myself "Now Bert, if you just pulled a few switches . . ." The old ladies wouldn't be able to see their prayer books. No one would hear the canon-in-residence, nor the precentor, nor the Archdeacon – not that that'd be much loss. The organ would stop however much Berwick waggled his fingers. And even the light in the Lantern would go out. What about that, then, Mr Treloar?'

'Very impressive,' murmured Septimus. 'I suppose this door goes into the crypt?'

'Yes,' Bert agreed. 'That's my private way. The quick way down when she blows a fuse.'

'Who keeps the key?' Septimus asked.

'I do, of course,' said Bert. 'But Harry Tulloch's got one as well – in his hole. Got a key to everything, has Harry.'

'Thank you, Bert,' said Septimus. 'Can I go back your quick way?'

Bert opened the door for him and ushered him into the crypt, the electric light from the workshop spilling a washed-out path of yellow on the grey stone of the floor. Once the door closed there was only a cold twilight from the small windows and the squat shadows of the great pillars like stone soldiers waiting in the gloom.

Septimus struck a match and held it high over his head, looking back at the wooden wall of the workshop. Now he had come in from the alley, the geography of the thing was much clearer. The workshop was part of a wooden box built against the north side of the crypt, a box divided into four compartments. From left to right they were first the steps coming down from the alley, then the electrician's workshop, third the junk store and fourth the bottom organ room. And the entrance to Bert's workshop had once been a crypt window. He used the last glimmer of the match to look at his watch, cursed briefly, and walked as quickly as he could towards the steps leading up into the nave. He was already ten minutes late for his appointment with the Archdeacon.

There were five men on the steps leading up to the Deanery front door. Mrs Wedge was standing in the doorway, one hand on the door, the other on the post. She was looking harassed. Her eye caught Septimus's over the heads of the little crowd, but he hurried on, pretending not to have seen. With his past experience, one glance had been enough. The five men were newspaper reporters. One figure detached itself from the bunch and followed him.

'Have you anything to say, Mr Treloar? I gather the ghost walked again last night.' It was the bearded Mr Jones. His black eye was now turning to sunset shades of purple and green.

'You'd better ask the ghost,' said Septimus, plunging into the shadow of the Peterport.

'Fine,' said Mr Jones. 'Can I quote you? "Ex-chief-inspector says the ghost exists." "Parson-Policeman Believes in Ghost." How about that for a headline?'

'I can suggest a better one,' said Septimus. 'How about "Parson-Policeman Assaults Reporter"?' John Jones stopped at the top of Chandlers Way and watched Septimus hurry down the hill. 'You pugilistic old man,' he shouted.

The Archdeacon's study was a curiously bare room with two imitation leather armchairs in front of an empty hearth. The floor was covered in linoleum in an imitation parquet pattern, and in one corner there was a large mahogany dining table with a mass of recording equipment on it. They sat on either side of the empty grate, instead of in the wide window where the view was the same as the Dean's. The Archdeacon poured coffee – surprisingly good coffee. Being, like Septimus, a bachelor, the Archdeacon had learned to do domestic things for himself, and being a stickler for efficiency, he did some of them rather well. The Archdeacon had been not a little frosty about Septimus's late arrival, but now he seemed curiously reluctant to come to the point of the interview. He asked ponderous questions about Septimus's parish, and very obviously did not listen to the answers. He cleared his throat dramatically two or three times, and finally stood up and went to fiddle with the recording equipment in the corner. He cleared his throat yet again, loudly and artificially.

'Treloar,' he said, 'I have come to a decision. An important decision.'

'Yes,' murmured Septimus without turning round. 'Do tell me.' Whatever extraordinary confession the Archdeacon was contemplating, he did not want to put the other man off by sounding too eager.

'Yes. I have decided . . That is . . . Listen to this.'

There was a click from the recording equipment on the table and then a tape started. It was a bad, very distant recording of Primrose's 'Suite for Janet'. Septimus turned to look. It was being played on the portable machine that the Archdeacon had used in the Minster.

'This is what happened on Monday night,' said the Archdeacon. 'First the playing of Primrose's music . . .' Septimus did not reply. He wondered if the recorder would be good enough to have picked up the noises that John Jones had made when he ran in panic along the clerestory.

'Then footsteps,' said the Archdeacon. And there they were, surprisingly clear on the tape. Septimus kept his own counsel about the footsteps. It would be interesting to see what the Archdeacon was driving at.

'Now listen carefully,' said the Archdeacon. In the very far distance, behind the music and the footsteps, they heard a voice cry, 'Don't! Don't!' Septimus smiled remembering the shout he had given and how it had seemed to echo in the building. Now it sounded like a ghost pleading for mercy.

'Primrose pleading for mercy,' said the Archdeacon. Septimus gulped at the unexpected identification and the way the Archdeacon's words had voiced his own thought.

The Archdeacon switched off the recorder and started to walk up and down the room, his hands clasped behind his back.

'Treloar, I must ask you – in the strictest confidence of course – have you come to any conclusion about this business?'

'No,' said Septimus without hesitation.

'Well, I have. I can truthfully say that I have. Though tonight and tomorrow will prove all.'

'Yes,' said Septimus. 'Tell me.' He was startled and fascinated.

'As you know,' said the Archdeacon as if he was about to begin a lecture, 'I have devoted much of my life to psychic research. Sadly, but perhaps inevitably in a fallen world, much of that time has been expended – wasted – in the exposure of fraud. Yet for all the deceit there are strong precedents for believing that there are more things than are dreamt of in a policeman's philosophy. Treloar. As you well know, we have Biblical warrant for such belief. There is King Saul and the – ah – Witch of Endor . . .' Septimus's head was turned away so that the Archdeacon could not see his lips twitch.

'. . . There is the evidence of Our Lord who cast out evil spirits. There is the evidence of Saint Paul . . .' He went on in this way for quite a long time. He quoted Saint Clement, and an obscure work called *The Revelation of Eusebius* of which Septimus had never heard. He talked about the Anglo-Saxon monster Grendel, and he quoted Chaucer, Camden, Shakespeare, and Sir Arthur Conan Doyle. It was a masterly survey. Septimus understood about half of it and believed rather less.

At last the Archdeacon came to the point. 'So,' he said, 'I began my investigation of this case in a spirit of scepticism, but as the affair has proceeded, I have changed my mind.' That made Septimus jump. The Archdeacon was saying that he now believed in the ghost!

'There are three classic starting points,' continued the Archdeacon, '– what one might call "triggers" – for a real spirit manifestation. One is violence. The second a strong attachment to a place. The third an equally strong attachment to an ordered time sequence – as the vulgar believe, the ghost of the murdered man walks where he met his death and on the anniversary of his death.' He stopped lecturing and pacing and turned earnestly to Septimus. 'It is my belief that these three conditions are supremely fulfilled in the case we are considering . . .' He held up his hand to prevent Septimus interrupting. 'I am persuaded that we have witnessed the tentative beginnings of the re-enactment of the tragedy. Consider. Here we have Primrose murdered almost exactly two hundred years ago. Two hundred years ago tomorrow night, to be precise. And this at the very moment when his grave is uncovered. Now had there already been an exact reconstruction of the murder, like you, Treloar, I should still suspect fraud. But this has not been the case. This week we have witnessed a re-enactment struggling to be born. A re-enactment which you yourself cannot explain by natural causes. You have set traps and so have I. Yet our traps have remained unsprung. So I have come to the conclusion that we are witnessing the spiritual echo of Primrose's tragedy two hundred years after the event.' He fell silent, looking at Septimus, who did not reply as a series of apparently unrelated pictures passed through his mind. Lovebody's Journal open on the library table in the middle of the night. Ted Barnes producing the book from his tool bag. Alisdair playing the recording of the 'Suite for Janet'. A lantern in the clerestory which seemed to come from the wrong direction. A gap beside the organ pipes. The crypt door closed when it should have been open. Septimus had spent most of his life investigating villainy and if this was a genuine haunting he would eat his clerical collar. He came back to the present, realizing that the Archdeacon was demanding some sort of answer.

'Very interesting,' he said. 'Can you prove it in the particular case?'

'I think so,' said the Archdeacon, picking up a sheaf of notes from the table. 'There is a marked correlation between the events of the last week and the details in Lovebody's Journal.' He consulted the notes. 'For last Monday Lovebody records that he heard the organ. That was the night I heard it myself with Tulloch and Barnes. The next night we heard the organ again, and Jancey's footsteps in the clerestory, and Primrose crying "don't". For that night Lovebody only records the organ. The footsteps and, of course, the cry, come later. As I would expect from my experience, the sequence is not yet in proper order. For the next night Lovebody makes no entry, and – so far as I know – nothing happened in the Minster on that night – which was Wednesday. Last night we heard the organ again, and saw the lantern. Lovebody records both – plus the footsteps, which – of course – we did not hear. So the event becomes more exact as the week proceeds. There remain tonight and tomorrow.'

'And what are we to expect tonight and tomorrow?' asked Septimus. The Archdeacon looked at him and then passed across his notes.

'Read it for yourself,' he said.

August 13th. Tonight the sea light extinguished. The night is wrong, for it should have been tomorrow. They should not have buried him where they did, for that is the way the other comes, and I am persuaded it draws him. The dead over the grave of the dead. And to what assignation? Mercy. Mercy. Mercy.

August 15th. It is ended. Last night I saw him, and he looked at me, and him in his grave these ten months.

I was drawn by the playing. So gay the music, but my heart cold with terror. I stood within the doorway. God help me, I could no other, and the music a dance of the damned. He came. I saw him on the walkway. He is bigger than I thought, for I never saw him in life, and he is bearded and in his sea clothes. And he looked on me, his face livid from the rope. And he knew my part in it. So they played out their devil's play. Primrose screamed as he died. I had not thought of that, and there is but one end for me who am guilty as hell itself . . .

13   Chase in the Crypt

Septimus walked slowly up Chandlers Way thinking out the implications of all that the Archdeacon had said. He was totally unconvinced by the theory which seemed to him half wishful-thinking and half a mis-reading of the evidence. Anyway, there were a number of facts which clearly pointed to a human agency. Lovebody's Journal for instance. Had the ghost put that in the Lantern? The Archdeacon had simply dismissed this as a piece of foolery irrelevant to the main issue. Septimus was not so prepared to dismiss it. It had got there somehow. He corrected himself with habitual caution. At least, it had disappeared from the library. He himself had never actually seen it in the Lantern. This started a train of thought that kept him going for some moments. Then there was the matter of the closed crypt door. Septimus had not told the Archdeacon about that. Indeed, the more the Archdeacon had elaborated his theory, the more reticent Septimus had become. The step between wanting something to be true and taking steps to make it come true was not all that large. And the Archdeacon was knowledgeable about tape recorders. And Bert Smith the electrician did a lot of work for him. And Bert had overhauled the public address system. Admittedly that had been before the Archdeacon had joined the Minster staff – or so Bert had said. And that was something that would bear investigating.

He turned to a consideration of what the Archdeacon said

was going to happen during the coming two nights. Tonight the Lantern would be extinguished. Tomorrow, the two hundredth anniversary of the murder, the whole tragedy would be re-enacted. The Archdeacon – with unusual humility – had discussed his plans with Septimus. He wanted to take measures to ensure against fraud, and for the rest he intended to watch the re-enactment. Indeed, he hoped to photograph it. Septimus wrinkled his nose with distaste. He could see several gaping holes in the plans, the main one being the question of whom you could trust. Could you, for instance, trust the Archdeacon? Anyway, he would have to reserve judgement on that. The first thing was tonight's all-star attraction, the light in the Lantern. If he were a ghost, how would he set about extinguishing it? Pull out the fuse in Bert Smith's workshop? Switch it off in the Lantern itself? Septimus looked up at the Lantern, high on top of the Petertower. It glinted against a grey sky. But it told him nothing.

As he passed the Deanery Alisdair Cameron came out of the door.

'Holmes,' he said. 'The old man wants to see you. He's in a proper state. Reporters all over the place.'

The Dean was indeed in 'a state'. He was more rattled than Septimus had ever seen him, having been thoroughly hounded by the press.

'M-my dear Septimus,' he said, 'you really must detect to some purpose. And soon. I feel like the Witch of Endor m-myself. Only she did not have to contend with the Jerusalem M-mirror.'

'Thirty-six hours,' said Septimus, 'and I'll lay your ghost. Until then I can only suggest that you arm the vergers and instruct them to shoot journalists on sight.'

The Dean smiled for the first time. 'I had thought of that,' he said. 'I am also thinking of locking the Peterport and we haven't done that since the Napoleonic War.' The Dean was, of course, joking. But it was a joke that came true.

That night after evensong when Harry Tulloch and Ted Barnes locked the Minster they were not armed with shotguns, though Harry wished they were, for they flushed no less than three reporters from various hiding places, and two of them had to be dislodged a second time from subsidiary hiding places in the cloister. And when all appeared at last to be peaceful, Septimus, making his own tour of inspection, ιw the altar frontal in the Saint Aidan chapel move in a ɔreeze when there was no breeze. Beneath the altar he discovered the enterprising John Jones. Ignoring that resourceful young man's voluble protests, and assisted by Harry, he marched him out of the building. Then Harry Tulloch went to the Dean. He was in a considerable temper. 'Begging your pardon, sir,' he said. 'Pigeons I can cope with, and owls, and jackdaws. Even cockroaches – as you well know from the plague we had last year. But journalists!' So the Dean ordered the door of the Peterport to be closed and locked, which was hard luck on Bert Smith who lived in the Gate House and had the job of opening up for anyone who had lawful reason for going into Cloister Garth.

So the journalists, having achieved what only Napoleon had managed before them, retreated to the Master Mariner and were reduced to swapping large gins for small stories from Ma Wenlock.

As night closed in Septimus wandered round the great building, eating a pork pie and keeping a weather eye open for any stray reporters who might have been overlooked. He had changed into his old clothes and was feeling relaxed and at ease. Answers to the questions 'how?' and 'why?' were beginning to take shape in his mind. They were too indistinct for him to be clear about 'who?', but if he was sure about anything, he was certain that tonight the ghost would extinguish the Lantern. As the Archdeacon said, it would have to happen, because tomorrow was the two hundredth anniversary of Primrose's murder. It would have to happen because Lovebody's Journal had been found in the Lantern, and because there had been no trace of the ghostly music on Mary Crowle's tape recorder. He paused at the chancel steps, gazing up through the gathering darkness at the clerestory where it vanished behind the organ, thinking about the light which he and the Archdeacon had seen. He had said to himself that it had come from the east instead of from the west – which would have been right for the haunting. But that was not an accurate statement. He grinned to himself. You might disbelieve the re-enactment of a murder, but that did not stop you being influenced by the story. He concentrated. The accurate thing to say was that the lantern had not come from the west. It could have come from the east ... or up ... or down. No, not down – that would have been visible. He stuffed the remainder of his pie into his mouth and went up the organ steps into the clerestory. It was dark behind the pipes, but framed in the arch he could see the angels who crowned the instrument. They looked gay and abandoned, as if they were about to dive into the choir.

He shone his torch up into the arch. Immediately above the gap at the end of the row of big pipes there was a hook let into the stone, and there was a pulley block hanging from it. He stood dangerously on the balustrade. The hook looked old, the pulley new, although both were painted grey so that you would not see them against the grey stone unless you were looking for them. He moved the torch from side to side and in its beam he caught a glint of thread, like the gleam of a spider's web in sunlight. He brought the torch down the thread and felt with his hand across the empty space. There was a nylon thread, a very thin fishing line looped over the pulley. It disappeared down through the space by the largest of the organ pipes. He guessed that it went right down to the crypt.

It did. It took him some moments to locate the bottom of the fishing line in the lower organ room, but eventually he found it. Both ends were looped round an insignificant tack. He undid them, tied one end round his torch and hauled it up between the pipes, watching it as it went, swaying and dipping, rotating, lighting up the roof of the crypt, then the upper organ room, then the long smooth sweep of the big pipes, and finally the grey stone of the clerestory. Satisfied, he lowered the torch, untied it, and returned the two ends of the line to the tack.

Next, using Harry Tulloch's key, he let himself into the electrician's workshop. He located the fuse-box for the Lantern and began to trace the cable. It ran along the wooden partition and then dived through a hole into the crypt. Then it ran along the outside of the partition, along the stone wall and finally disappeared into the floor of the nave. He could not find where it emerged, so he went to the other end, all the way up to the Lantern itself, and traced the cable back down the wall of the circular stairs until it disappeared into a conduit at the bottom. Septimus considered the matter. If he was a ghost and proposing to extinguish the Lantern he would do it from the switchboard. He collected his gear from his hidey-hole beneath the organ and went down to Bert Smith's workshop. He made himself as comfortable as he could with two upright chairs. He turned off the light and left the door into the crypt ajar. It was not long before he was asleep.

It was not often that Septimus dreamed, but that night, he did. He dreamed about thunder and lightning. It was late autumn and he was in the churchyard of Danedyke Saint

Mary's. He was cutting the grass with one of the Archdeacon's tape recorders, and the Archdeacon himself was watching his progress from the top of a stone tomb with 'Hezekiah Primrose' printed on newspaper on the side of it. Harry Tulloch, using a vacuum-cleaner, was helping him with the mowing, while Ted and Norman Barnes were riding up and down the path on Norman's motor cycle. Ted had an aerial erected on Norman's crash helmet and was broadcasting to Tokyo about Septimus Treloar haunting the Minster. And all the while there was a thunderstorm rumbling overhead. Mary Crowle came through the lych gate carrying the school tape recorder. The thunder rumbled and the lightning flashed. Ted Barnes jumped off the back of the motor bike and took the recorder from Mary Crowle. It started to rain, great drops of water falling like blood on the tombstones. Septimus was thinking, 'about time to stop'. Ted Barnes put the recorder on top of the tomb at the feet of the Archdeacon. He opened the lid and altered the controls. 'Now the music will start,' thought Septimus but it did not. Ted turned, and he had a lantern in his hand, and as he turned there was a great clap of thunder and a flash of lightning reaching down from the heavens to the Archdeacon's clerical trilby. The Archdeacon crumbled into a little pile of dust on top of the tomb and Septimus woke up with a start.

It was dark in the workshop, but despite the dream Septimus knew that something external had awakened him. There was no sound or light. But there was something ... There was a smell. He wrinkled his nose, trying to identify it. Beaches ... ozone ... insulation. That was it! It was an electrical smell! He slid out of his sleeping bag, torch in hand, and ran up the steps and out into the alley. It was dark outside. The cold night air completed his awakening. The Lantern was extinguished. Below it the clock in the Peter-tower said that it was ten to three.

Swiftly he went back into the workshop. After the night air the electrical smell was much more pronounced. He went to the switchboard and pulled out the fuse for the Lantern. As he expected, it was burnt out. He went to the door leading into the crypt, eased it open, and stood there listening, his eyes searching the blackness. It was no more than forty seconds since he had slid out of his sleeping bag.

It was absolutely still in the crypt. Not merely quiet, but a total absence of all sound. Darkness and silence, like a soft blanket which one could touch.

So Septimus stood, aware of the one sound which was the thumping of his own heart. The seconds crawled by and grew into minutes and still Septimus stood, motionless as the invisible pillars of the crypt. Then, at last, his patience was rewarded. There was a swift scuffle of movement in the blackness. It was cut off as suddenly as it came. It was not a mouse or a rat. A human being had moved somewhere in the blackness of the crypt. Septimus pointed the torch, trying to gauge the direction of the sound. The beam stabbed out in the blackness illuminating a stark perspective of pillars and arches. They seemed dazzling white in the sudden light, and they threw a herring bone of black shadows. In the very edge of the beam there was a flicker of movement. Septimus swung the torch, and momentarily there was the figure of a man. The torch beam caught him for a second, and then he was gone into the shadowy maze of pillars. A man dressed in black, his face white as leprosy in the torchlight. Septimus could hear his footsteps running, heedless now of noise, somewhere between the pillars in the surrounding darkness. He switched off the torch and waited and the age-old silence descended once again. Septimus frowned in the darkness, knowing he must do something – and quickly. There were two ways out of the crypt, and he was covering one of them. But there were the steps up into the nave, and among the pillars you would never catch anyone by the light of a torch. Septimus pulled the workshop door closed behind him. The click of the lock was loud in the silence. He moved carefully forward in what he judged was the direction of the nave steps. After about twenty paces he blundered into a pillar and had to use the torch. The brief stab of the beam produced a scuffle of movement which, he judged, came from somewhere behind him. He swung the torch round slowly, feeling terribly vulnerable, like a rabbit lost in the middle of a stone forest, pillars and shadows wheeling in the beam of the torch, going away into blackness in every direction. By the light of the torch he identified the wooden wall of the workshop, turned through one hundred and eighty degrees and shone the torch down a long avenue of stone. There at the end was the arched shadow of the bottom of the steps. On the wall beside the arch he could see the switches for the crypt lights. Keeping the torch on now, he ran down the avenue, conscious as he did so of movement behind him. But he did not turn. There was nothing to be done about the intruder until he had switched the lights on.

He reached the arch and clicked the switches watching as the light sprang up in patches all over the crypt, revealing long perspectives of pillar and arch.

He searched the crypt methodically, going from wall to wall down each avenue of pillars, looking to left and right and behind as he went. But there was no sign of the intruder. He carefully searched the bottom organ room and the store next to it. But there was no one hiding behind the bellows or among the mouldering hassocks. So it came down to the electrician's workshop. Whoever it had been must have a key to the yale lock on the door. It would have been easy to slip round behind him as he went across to the switches. For a moment Septimus toyed with the idea of continuing the search outside. After all, the Dean had locked the Peterport.

He put the idea regretfully aside. There must be a dozen places where you could climb the walls, certainly there were a hundred where you could hide. Without an army it would be impossible to search the precincts of the Minster.

He went back into the workshop and had a closer look at the fuse for the Lantern. The wire had disappeared altogether, leaving a black stain on the porcelain. Evidently the short circuit had been dramatic and complete. He went back into the crypt and followed the cable along the wall, examining it closely by the light of the torch.

Where the cable turned upward to disappear under the floor of the nave there was a junction box. Septimus unscrewed the cap and shone his torch inside. One of the brass terminals was twisted and misshapen – partially melted. He nodded to himself. That was how it had been done – the blade of a screwdriver held between the two terminals … flash! It would do the screwdriver no good at all, but it would certainly extinguish the light in the Lantern.

Septimus started a reconstruction. So … the intruder had come down from the nave. He stopped and checked back. The Peterport was locked. So either the intruder lived in Cloister Garth or he had found a way to climb in. He had entered the nave by the south door and so had come down to the crypt. He had blown the fuse with his screwdriver and then – disturbed by Septimus – he had escaped through the workshop. But if he carried a key to the workshop why had he not come in that way? Septimus had no manner of doubt that the ghost was perfectly aware that he himself was sleeping in the Minster under the organ. So why risk coming through the nave? Or did he know that Septimus was spending the night in Bert Smith's workshop? And if so, how? Septimus had told no one. He had not even seen anyone since he had made up his mind to do so. He frowned. There was something about this that did not add up. It was like a jigsaw puzzle which had collected half a dozen pieces from a totally different puzzle. At the edge of his mind, like the intruder whom he had seen so briefly in the light of his torch, there was a perfectly simple explanation of the whole puzzle. It was like a well-known name on the tip of his tongue. But he could not produce it. He gave up, hoping as one does with a name, that the answer would come when he was not thinking about it. He replaced the cover on the junction box and went back to his sleeping bag.

14 The Archdeacon Lays a Plan

Septimus awoke because someone was shaking his shoulder. He opened one eye and groaned. The bench against which he was leaning was unbelievably hard, and he appeared to be dead from the waist down.

'Come along, Treloar. It is nearly eight o'clock, and I have prepared breakfast for both of us.' Septimus got a face into focus, a long face with a smile like a whinnying horse and the sharp white line of a clerical collar ruled across the bottom of it. He closed one eye and groaned again. He really could not cope with the Archdeacon at eight o'clock in the morning, and the thought of breakfast with him was too horrific to contemplate.

'Now, wakey, wakey, as I believe they say in Her Majesty's Navy.'

Septimus was shocked into opening both eyes. The Archdeacon was being coy and he was obviously very pleased about something. Septimus struggled, muttering, out of his sleeping bag. The Archdeacon was clad in neat clerical grey. He was shaven like the priest in the nursery rhyme, and he smelt of after-shave lotion. Septimus, passing a hand across his scrubby chin, decided that in all his life he had never seen anything so revolting.

'I was right,' said the Archdeacon, grinning like a fox saying good morning to a turkey. 'I said the Lantern would be extinguished. And behold! It was.'

'The fuse blew,' Septimus growled.

'But of course! You can hardly expect a spirit to turn off a switch.'

Septimus grunted sourly. You could hardly expect a spirit to take the cover off a junction box and lay a screwdriver between the terminals. But as far as he was concerned, the Archdeacon could have his fun. He ran a hand through his tousled hair and tried to smile.

'Lead me to this breakfast,' he said. He almost sounded as if he meant it.

Breakfast was not one of the Archdeacon's specialities, and so far as Septimus was concerned the meal was an almost total disaster. The only saving feature was the coffee, which was every bit as good as yesterday's had been. Later on, Septimus decided that it was only the coffee which prevented him from dramatically cutting his throat with the Archdeacon's blunt bread knife. He stared into a grey pool of lumpy porridge, its steam wafting round his ears like the vapour coming out of a drain, and he thought longingly of the pool of his own heart's blood on the Archdeacon's practical linoleum. The porridge was succeeded by a kipper which the Archdeacon had boiled as determinedly as if he were trying to reduce it to glue. It lay in front of Septimus in a sinister puddle on a willow-pattern plate looking like something the cat had found in a dustbin the local council had never discovered. Septimus shuddered visibly and helped himself to a piece of toast. He tried to break it but it bent happily through one hundred and eighty degrees like a piece of rubberized roofing felt. Hysterically he waggled it back and forth. How did you get toast into that state? Soak it in impact adhesive and steam it in a slow oven? He began to invent a fantasy about the toast. The Archdeacon could patent it as a new form of floor tile for public lavatories; or you could use it to bind a copy of Lovebody's Journal . . .

'. . . and I suggest that you stay in the clerestory at the top of the organ steps, since you are our policeman and that is the focal point.'

Septimus was bumped abruptly into the present. The Archdeacon had been going over his plans for the coming night, and Septimus had attended to none of them.

'Go through that again, so I'm sure I've got it clear,' he said, cuddling his coffee, really concentrating now.

Grudgingly he admitted that the Archdeacon had now got it all sewn up. All the doors into the Minster were to be locked and the Archdeacon was having bolts fitted on the inside. Ted Barnes was to be posted at the top of the Peter-steps, Harry Tulloch was to be with the Archdeacon and Septimus was to have the place of honour in the clerestory beside the organ loft.

'But why not you?' asked Septimus. 'I should have thought you would have wanted to be the first to shake Captain Jancey by the hand – or whatever one does socially on meeting a ghost.'

The Archdeacon frowned. 'There is no need to be frivolous, Treloar. I wish to observe the whole phenomenon from the nave. Indeed, I hope to take some photographs. If I manage it, it will set the coping stone on twenty years of endeavour.'

Septimus, because at this stage he could do little else, promised to play his part and so escaped from the disastrous breakfast.

Fifty yards above the Archdeacon's house there was a seat in Chandlers Way. Septimus collapsed gratefully on to it, thinking about the Archdeacon's plans and wondering what he was going to do about them. He looked up at the Lantern. The glass was flashing in the morning sun. Well, it had gone out as the Archdeacon has said it would do. His eye travelled down from the Lantern, down the grey hulk of the Peter-tower and along the line of the clerestory windows to where he was supposed to be spending the night. There in the clerestory, behind the first of the windows hidden from view by the Cottages.

Abruptly he shot to his feet. The clerestory window immediately behind the organ! You could not see it from Chandlers Way. The thing was clearly impossible. Yet on Thursday night Ted Barnes had come into the Minster because he claimed to have seen the light through that window. It could have been no other window because the light had never moved along the clerestory at all. As he had proved to his own satisfaction, it had been hauled up from the crypt. Therefore Ted had been lying. Therefore ... A whole series of unformed suspicions gradually crystallized in Septimus's mind. He was so engrossed that without noticing what he was doing he climbed on to the Archdeacon's garden wall and stood there gazing intently at the clerestory. The torrent of his thoughts streamed on. Ted had not seen the light, but he knew it was there. Therefore he must have arranged it himself from the inside. There would have been time to work the lantern from the crypt and then go out through Bert Smith's workshop and round the west end of the minster and so in at the south door. Then he remembered the man who had been in the crypt last night. How had he got in? Not through Bert Smith's workshop because Septimus had been sleeping there. There was a simpler explanation – something to do with the fact that the entrance to Bert's workshop had once been a window. It nagged at his mind for a full minute and then with what seemed like an audible click everything fell into place. It was like the pattern of a kaleidoscope when you stop moving it. Of course! That was how it was done, and that was who was doing it, and with an imaginative leap of sympathy he could make a pretty shrewd guess as to why it was being done. Then he remembered the Archdeacon's elaborate plans, and he suddenly realized that he sympathized with the hoax, and he knew with absolute certainty that if he took up his planned position in the clerestory that night, the ghost of John Jancey simply would not walk. So he would have to disappear efficiently and publicly, leaving the Archdeacon with Harry and Ted in control of the Minster.

He felt a determined tug at his trouser leg and came back to the present to find a boy gazing up at him.

'What are you looking at mister?' Septimus realized that he was surrounded by a small crowd, some of whom were searching the grey lines of the Minster, some of whom were gazing at him like cows round a tree.

Septimus grinned engagingly at the boy.

'I thought I saw the ghost in the Lantern,' he said, and as all eyes swivelled to the top of the Petertower, he climbed off the wall and made his escape up Chandlers Way.

Alisdair Cameron answered the Deanery door to Septimus. Yes, of course he could use the telephone, and the Dean was out at a Mothers' Union Rally and not expected back until after dinner.

Septimus allowed Alisdair to come into the Dean's study with him, firmly closing the door to prevent Mrs Wedge from overhearing.

'Watson, I'm hatching a plot, and you're part of it. So you can sit down on the sofa and listen.'

He sat at the Dean's desk considering, his hand on the telephone. He was going to ring his closest friend, Chief Inspector Sam Burroughs. It was Saturday, so unless he was out on a case Sam would be at home.

He rang Sam's home, an Esher number, and after a moment got Mary Burroughs on the line. She sounded delighted to hear his voice.

'Yes. Sam's in the garden. He's concreting the drive. I'll get him.' There was a pause, and then Sam's well-remembered voice. 'Damn. I'm concreting the telephone.'

'Sam,' said Septimus, 'are you burying a corpse under all that concrete? Very suspicious I call it.'

'Yes,' said Sam, 'I just murdered H.M. Tax Vulture. And I know what you're up to, you horrible no-parson. Saw it in the papers. Running a con with an inflatable plastic ghost, that's what you're doing. Where the action is – there is the septic reverend.'

It was fun. They slipped so easily into the old banter.

'And what can I do for the Church Militant?' asked Sam.

'Sam. I am investigating this ghost business. And I've reached the stage where I must disappear from the scene with a loud noise and publicly.'

'You could always burst,' suggested Sam unhelpfully, 'or immolate yourself on a cathedral coke stove. Do it as a protest against Today's Dissolute Youth.'

'Stop being a clot,' said Septimus, 'and try to be a helpful, keen and intelligent detective.' There was a squawk and a mutter of conversation at the other end of the line, then Sam said, 'No. That wasn't me being helpful, intelligent and keen. Mary just brought me some coffee. So go on, Septimus – I'm all ears.'

'Well. For the purposes of this exercise, you're my brother-in-law.'

'Good God!' said Sam.

'You're married to my sister,' said Septimus firmly, 'and in half an hour I want you to ring this number. Minster Saint Peter 263 . . .'

'Half a mo while I write that down,' said Sam.

'It's the Deanery,' continued Septimus, 'but the Dean's out, so you'll get his housekeeper, Mrs Wedge . . . No! Not Hedge. Wedge . . . Yes Wedge. My sister – your wife, Sam –

she's suffered a cataclysm. Struck by lightning or given birth to a three-headed calf. She's got rabies and the vet despairs of her life. And I'm to come to Esher at once. That's the point. Is that clear?'

'Couldn't be clearer, old son. I can see the Black Death stalking up the drive, putting his bony feet into my wet concrete.'

'But Mrs Wedge, she won't know where I am. So you are to say that you know I've been working with the Archdeacon, the Venerable Aloysius Jenkins . . .'

'Repeat that,' said Sam. Septimus did so.

'I don't believe it,' said Sam. 'Nobody could have a name like that. It isn't in reason.'

'The Venerable Aloysius Jenkins,' said Septimus severely. 'Mrs Wedge will then give you his phone number, and you will ring him with your convincing tale of woe.'

'He will then tell you,' said Sam, 'and the Venomous Septic Treloar will burst into tears and disappear in the theoretical direction of Esher with a loud bang and a nasty smell.'

'That's it,' said Septimus.

'I suppose it doesn't mean you could really come down to Esher?' asked Sam hopefully. 'We can always lock up the silver and we'd love to see you.'

'Afraid not,' Septimus said.

'Thought it would be a horrid fraud. I suppose you're going to lurk under the dirty surplices in the vestry?'

'Yes, I'm going to lurk. But I will come down when it's all over, Sam. Promise. Interesting case. First case I've ever investigated where nobody's broken the law – at least, not so's you'd notice.'

They said their goodbyes and Septimus hung up. He turned to Alisdair.

'Now then, Watson, you heard what I said to Sam, so let's

make ourselves scarce until after he's rung. You come-along-of-me.' They went out into the hall, and Septimus called to the housekeeper.

'Mrs Wedge, I'm taking Alisdair out for lunch if that's all right. I thought we'd drive along the coast.'

They collected the landrover and drove out to Septimus's lonely beach on the Home Farm land, going via the Bluebell to collect pies and pop and beer. The sky was grey, the wind feathering the sea with flecks of white. They lay on the sand and ate and drank and watched birds through Septimus's binoculars, and the priest told the boy what he wanted him to do that night.

'I can do better than a rope,' Alisdair said. 'I've got a rope ladder in my tree house in the garden.'

'Much better,' said Septimus, remembering his last efforts with a rope. 'I'm getting a bit mossy green for playing Tarzan.'

'Can I come with you?' asked Alisdair wistfully. 'Into the Minster, I mean?'

Septimus's heart went out to the lonely boy. He decided he must be getting sentimental in his dotage.

'Yes,' he said at last, 'I don't see why not. If your father didn't have me unfrocked for being drunk and disorderly, I don't suppose he will for taking you on a ghost hunt in the middle of the night. Two things, though. It'll probably look extremely creepy, so you're to remember it's all a hoax, and whatever you do, you're to keep your mouth shut. You can't come if you have hysterics when the ghost walks. Promise?'

'Yes,' Alisdair replied, 'I promise.'

'Second thing. When the show's over I shall have to go and have words with the actors. Now you positively can't come on that in case there's a barney. So when I tell you, will you go straight home to bed?'

Alisdair grinned. He was fond of the big priest and saw the logic of what he was saying.

'Not even if I bring my revolver, Holmes?'

'Not even if you bring your revolver, Watson.'

When they got back to Minster Saint Peter they called on the Archdeacon. Septimus had a specious excuse ready in case anything had gone wrong with the plot, but it proved unnecessary.

The Archdeacon beamed at him, and then remembering that he was the bearer of ill tidings, he switched to the lugubrious glower he used for news of death and disaster.

'Ah, Trcloar. I've been sending out forage parties for you to the far corners of the county. I have bad news for you, I fear. Your brother-in-law rang.'

'What, Sam?' said Septimus in surprise.

'Yes. From Esher. Now you must steady yourself, Treloar . . .'

Septimus duly steadied himself. He looked like a blue-eyed bear whose honey bees have suddenly turned into wasps.

'You must go to Esher immediately. I fear your sister has been involved in a serious accident.'

'Oh!' said Septimus. The bear was about to burst into tears.

'Yes. According to Mr Burroughs, Primrose drove the Rolls head on into a – ah – dustcart. She has damaged her epiglottis badly.'

'Oh!' said Septimus again. Trust Sam to lumber him with a sister called Primrose, and only someone who had heard Sam talking officially about death and disaster could credit him with getting away with a story about a Rolls and a dustcart and a damaged epiglottis. And what on earth was an epiglottis?

'Alisdair!' said the Archdeacon angrily, 'this is no time to laugh. Think of Mr Treloar's feelings and his sister's epiglottis.'

'I'm sorry sir. I know I shouldn't laugh. It was just the bit about the dustcart.' Septimus looked frostily at Alisdair.

'Young man, when you are as old as the Archdeacon, you won't find anything funny about a dustcart.' He turned back to the other man. 'I'm sorry I won't be able to help you tonight, sir. But obviously I must drive straight down to Esher.'

'Of course, Treloar, of course. You have my sympathy, and indeed my prayers. And I will give you a full report when you return.'

When they were outside the house Septimus grinned at Alisdair. 'Watson, if you're going to be a detective, you'll have to learn to keep a straight face. Laughing at Primrose's epiglottis. I'm surprised at you, really I am.'

Septimus parted with Alisdair at the Deanery and went on into the Minster. He found Harry Tulloch in his cubby-hole polishing the processional cross.

'Harry, I've got to miss the Archdeacon's party tonight. I've got to go down to Esher. My sister's been involved in a car smash.'

Harry did not look up from his polishing. 'Major, you ain't got no sister. Don't you remember? You told me that night in the cave above Hjoda when we thought Jerry would get us in the morning, certain sure.'

He rubbed his thumb across the enamel in the middle of the cross and continued, 'Adam, he got killed at Alamein. Secundus, he went down in the *Hood*. Tertius and Quartus, the twins, they run a pottery in Brixham. Quintus – he's the bank manager – "God help him", that was what you said. And Sextus – he scarpered to Australia before the law caught up with him.' He breathed on the enamel and began to rub it with his cloth. 'So you ain't got no sister. Not unless your parents were more prolific than I ever heard of.'

'Harry,' said Septimus firmly, 'put down that duster and listen to me. For the purposes of this exercise I've got a sister. And what's more she's called Primrose. And you can take that grin off your face, Tulloch. She lives in Esher, and she's been involved in a smash between a Rolls and a dust-cart. All right, laugh if you want to. But that's what the Archdeacon believes. And if you give him any cause to doubt it, Harry Tulloch – I'll stuff that processional cross blunt end down your epiglottis.'

Harry controlled his mirth with some difficulty.

'And Harry . . . for the Archdeacon's party tonight I was supposed to be in the clerestory at the top of the organ steps. Now whatever happens, you're *not* to take my place. If any-body goes up there it must be Ted Barnes. Nobody but Ted. Understand?'

'Yes,' said Harry. 'Why?'

'If anyone but Ted's in that clerestory, the ghost won't walk. And that's a fact.'

'Fair enough,' said Harry. 'So while Ted and me help Himmler to lay this flippin' ghost, you drive to Esher?'

'That's it,' said Septimus.

'And where's Esher, Major? In the Song School, hiding behind the surplices?'

15 The Ghost of John Jancey

Septimus strolled slowly along the beach in the gathering darkness. It was chilly, with a gusty wind and a hint of rain in the air. Apart from a courting couple walking hand in hand at the water's edge and a tramp under the pier, there was no one to see him. It is doubtful if anyone would have recognized him. He was dressed in a moth-eaten fur hat – black and vaguely cossack-shaped – and a mac which was perhaps grubbier than that of the tramp. Beneath the mac he wore an old pair of slacks, a black roll-top sweater, and on his feet he had an old pair of black gym shoes.

He had made as public as possible his departure for Esher, then he had driven ten miles out on the London road before turning across country back to Danedyke Saint Mary's. He had gone straight to Tom Barton's garage so that he did not have to go into the village. He had had an uproarious supper with Tom and Rosemary and then driven back to Minster Saint Peter in Rosemary's car. He left the car in the public park at the far end of the beach, and then walked along the beach until he was immediately beneath the great bulk of the Minster. Apart from fishermen who would not know him, there were hardly likely to be any locals on the beach on a chilly August evening. He turned inland, over the shingle to the private beach steps of the Chandlers Way houses. The tramp was out of sight now, the courting couple engrossed with one another. Softly he opened the gate and stepped into the Archdeacon's garden. The house was in darkness, for the daily woman would have gone home long ago and the Archdeacon would already be in the Minster. Septimus went round the house and stood in the front porch. Across Chandlers Way he could see the gable end of the Deanery, the battlemented garden wall and the east end of the Minster itself.

The clock in the Petertower chimed ten-thirty. It was the hour of his rendezvous with Alisdair Cameron. Septimus reckoned that by now the night's haul of journalists would have been ejected from the Minster and would be safely ensconced in the Master Mariner, having 'one for the road' before taking up their chilly vigil in Chandlers Way. He supposed that there were such creatures as teetotal journalists, although he had never actually met one.

A moment after the booming of the clock a light winked out from the battlements opposite. Septimus slipped out of the garden and across the road. There was no one in sight. Alisdair's rope ladder was in the shadow of a buttress. He climbed swiftly up and was greeted on the top of the wall by the boy. They took the rope ladder back with them to Alisdair's bedroom, and there they waited for an hour, talking softly. Alisdair was excited and full of questions, Septimus cautious and disinclined to answer. He was not quite sure what was planned for this, the two hundredth anniversary of the murder, and anyway, what was to be made public about the whole business was a matter for the Dean.

The window rattled in a gust of wind and they heard rain patter on the glass. Septimus frowned. Rain was something he had not taken into account. He did not think it could make any difference, but he was not sure. The Minster clock boomed eleven-thirty.

'Come on, Watson,' said Septimus. 'The game's afoot.'

He opened the window and stepped out into the gusty

rain blowing off the sea. It was black and cold after the light and warmth of the bedroom. The lights of the town shimmered below them, and above the Lantern was a golden glow against the dark sky.

They were down the stone steps into the Deanery garden, Alisdair leading the way. In the middle of the garden a small building loomed up on their right. Septimus felt Alisdair's hand on his midriff, holding him back.

'Potting shed,' the boy whispered. 'Keep to the left of the path or you'll kick over a pile of flower pots.'

Obediently Septimus moved to his left and the two of them crept through the garden and so came out in Cloister Garth. A few windows still glowed round the dark square. Mostly they were bedroom windows, although behind them the light over the Deanery front door was still shining out.

They turned right down the side of the Minster and started to move westward, keeping in the shadow of the building. As they turned there was a sudden clatter behind them, and Septimus gazed back across the garden. Briefly a light flashed out illuminating the corner of the potting shed.

'What was that?' whispered Alisdair.

'Someone fell over the flower pots,' Septimus replied. He thought for two seconds, and then, 'Alisdair. Quick and quiet as you can. Round the west end. Wait for me by the west door.' Without comment Alisdair was gone, and Septimus blessed him for not stopping to ask questions. He himself ran after Alisdair down the side of the Minster, a plan already forming in his mind.

He stopped after about a hundred feet where there was a heavy door between two of the buttresses. It was the outside entrance to the coke-hole. Quickly and as quietly as possible he withdrew the bolt and opened the door, taking up position behind it.

From the shelter of the door he peered along the side of the Minster. Buttress succeeded buttress, black against the Deanery porch light. For a long minute nothing happened. Then a head appeared round the end buttress. It was in silhouette, and it was bearded. It looked like a Victorian miniature. The head turned cautiously in the dim light, gazing round Cloister Garth. It was John Jones the reporter from the *Advertiser*.

Septimus saw him slide round the end buttress and disappear into its shadow. He drew back against the wall, drawing the door with him, leaving the entrance to the stoke-hole gaping wide so that the irritating Mr Jones could not possibly miss it. And if he did miss it? Well . . . he had already clobbered an Archdeacon in this case, and he was perfectly prepared to clobber a reporter. Certainly he was not prepared to have the haunting ruined by Mr Jones.

He waited, suddenly conscious of the waiting as a thing he had done many times in the past – in the police, and during the War. But there was a difference. His hand resting on the coke-hole door he identified the difference and smiled into the rain. He was not afraid.

He heard cautious steps coming along the path. They stopped. He eased his big body round the door. He put his right hand – so gently – in the middle of John Jones's back, and pushed. There was a yell, a thump and an avalanche of slithering coke. Septimus closed the door and bolted it. He waited for the avalanche to subside, his ear against the planks.

'Mr Jones,' he said gently, 'Mr Jones.' There was a rustle of coke and then a tremulous voice said, 'Yes?'

'Mr Jones, this is Septimus Treloar. There are two ways out of that coke-hole and they're both bolted. If you keep quiet until I come and let you out I promise you the exclusive story – if there is any story.'

There was a pause before the reporter replied,

'And what happens if I raise blue murder?'

Septimus's heart warmed to the journalist. He recovered quickly and his enterprise was splendid.

'Then you'll get chucked out of Cloister Garth, there won't be a story and I shall get the Dean to prosecute for illegal entry.'

'Prosecute if you like.'

'Not you,' said Septimus, 'I'll get him to prosecute the Managing Director of the Syndicate. Your editor wouldn't like that.'

There was a brief silence and then what sounded uncommonly like a chuckle.

'O.K., padre. I'll come quietly. Coke seems quite comfortable. But one thing – will the dust explode if I smoke?'

Septimus collected Alisdair from the shadows of the west door.

'What happened?' whispered Alisdair.

'Oh, just a reporter. I got rid of him. Come on.'

They rounded the corner and went down the alley on the north side, through the tunnel beneath the Petersteps and so to the door to Bert Smith's workshop. Septimus unlocked the door and stepped into the utter blackness at the top of the steps. As he turned to close the door behind Alisdair, so he saw a gleam of light beneath the other door at the bottom of the steps. There was someone with a torch in the workshop! He pushed Alisdair back into the alley, closed the door noiselessly, grabbed the boy and ran with him down the alley. 'Come on Alisdair!' he hissed. 'Run like hell.'

Together they pelted back the way they had come, down the alley and through the tunnel under the Petersteps. Once on the far side Septimus skidded to a halt and dragged the boy into the shelter of a buttress.

'What's the matter?' whispered Alisdair, his voice quavering.

'I'm not sure. I think we arrived at the stage door. It's the bloke who's playing the ghost getting ready for his cue. But there's nothing to be scared about. Absolute silence, Watson, until I tell you.'

Septimus was puzzled. He was pretty sure he knew how the ghost would get into the crypt, but he had not been expecting it to come out of the electrician's workshop. If it came out that way, how did it propose to get into the clerestory with all the Archdeacon's troops on guard? He gave it up and huddled against the buttress, one arm round Alisdair waiting for the ghost to pass. But no one came. The minutes crawled by, and no one passed their hiding place. Whoever had been in the workshop had vanished. At last Septimus peered round the buttress. There was nothing to see, only the gloomy alley and the blackness of the tunnel under the Petersteps.

On the other side of the wall which separated the alley from Chandlers Way there was a street light. It shone over the wall and gave a ghostly light to the side of the steeply climbing Petersteps. Because the rain made the metal shine, the street light glimmered on the rungs of the iron ladder which went up beside the tunnel entrance to the roof of the Petersteps. Of course! That was it! The ladder led to the roof, and the roof was on the level with the clerestory. You could not introduce a ghost into the clerestory until the Archdeacon had finished his inspection. And because of the rain you could not put your ghost on to the Petersteps roof until the last possible moment. A ghost that left puddles of real water on the walkway would convince no one, not even the Archdeacon. Septimus almost laughed aloud. According to Canon Lovebody, on this night two hundred years ago there had been something of a storm. He would be prepared to bet that John Jancey had not altered his time schedule because of a drop of rain.

Moving very carefully Septimus and Alisdair crept back down the alley. They got into the workshop without further incident. Septimus opened the door in the wooden wall and looked into the utter blackness of the crypt. He stood for some time, listening, straining his eyes through the darkness. There was no sign of any human being but themselves. He took Alisdair by the arm and led him cautiously between the invisible pillars. More by luck than anything else they managed to find the steps leading to the nave without having to use the torch.

By contrast with the absolute darkness of the crypt the nave seemed almost light as Septimus eased open the top door and they peeped round it, one head above the other. There was a subdued murmur of conversation and the faint glimmer of a torch from where the Archdeacon had set up his equipment in the centre of the aisle. Septimus could recognize Harry Tulloch's voice. That meant Ted Barnes was at the top of the organ steps. It was safe to move. He led Alisdair across to the hiding place by the bookstall, and there they waited, watching the dark clerestory on the north wall. The Minster clock boomed out, distant, high over their heads. Midnight. Like an uneasy spirit the wind prowled and lamented round the building, rattling windows, dashing rain against glass, as if seeking a way in out of the night.

The minutes crawled by. There was no light of torch from the aisle now, no sound of conversation. The curtains round the Bishop's throne stirred in a draught. There was a crack of timber from somewhere overhead. High above it the Minster clock gravely registered the quarter, its voice rising and falling in the wind.

With the dying of the last note of the clock the music came. Hezekiah Primrose's 'Suite for Janet'. Soft at first – the murmur of the sea in a great cave – but growing louder. This night it seemed no longer hesitant. It was triumphant, sure of itself, its trumpet notes proclaiming the beauty of a woman, the splendour of the flesh. Septimus put a big arm round Alisdair's shoulder and drew him close to the security of his own solid side. He could feel the boy quiver, though with excitement or fear he could not tell.

Suddenly, despite himself, Alisdair gasped. Far down the clerestory there was a faint glow of light. It was in one of the tunnels and was defined by the pointed arch so that it looked like a pale yellow spearhead. It flickered with shadows. Then the arch vanished and there was a dark figure moving along the clerestory, made tiny by the distance, but a figure carrying a lantern which threw weird shadows across glass and stone. The figure disappeared into the next tunnel, and immediately the watchers saw a second spearhead of light growing brighter as before, until the figure emerged again. So it moved eastward down the clerestory, swiftly, silently. And all the while Primrose's 'Suite for Janet' pealed triumphantly through the dark vault of the nave.

They could see the ghost better now. It seemed to be wearing a dark coat or cloak. The face was very white, gleaming in the lamplight, and above the leprous face was a big three-cornered hat.

Suddenly there was a scream – a human scream – and the sound of feet clattering down the organ steps. A man came running from the direction of the choir. He jumped the chancel steps in one bound and ran down the aisle.

'Control yourself, Barnes!' It was the Archdeacon's voice, cold, clipped, incisive.

'God, sir! You haven't seen its face.'

The human interruption changed nothing. Still the figure moved eastward, swift and sinister, and still the music pealed out. Now the ghost was coming to the last tunnel before the organ. Here it paused. It turned to the balustrade and leaned over, raising the lantern higher so that it shone direct on the white face. Alisdair bit his lip to prevent himself crying out. He turned his head sideways against the chest of the big man whose arm was round his shoulder. It was an appalling face. A face framed by the black hat above and the black beard below, and between them – nothing. There *was* no face. Just a whiteness that shimmered in the light like a bowlful of maggots. So the thing stood for a moment, the gay music surging around it. Then it turned with horrifying swiftness. Organ pipes, golden angels came into brief silhouette as it disappeared from view. The music continued for perhaps two seconds and then collapsed on a discordant jumble of wailing notes. A terrified scream went echoing through the building and the lantern was extinguished. Then there was nothing but silence and darkness.

16   Septimus and the Ghost

It was after one o'clock when, for the second time that night, Septimus walked past the great west door of the Minster. The rain had stopped and the wind was blowing the clouds to tatters so that there were a few lonely stars shining in a moonless sky. He walked quietly, from habit rather than from caution, humming a hymn tune as he went. He was relaxed, contented, with a premonitory tingle about the interview in front of him. It was the old feeling, the feeling he always got when the case was almost over and one had only to tie up the ends and deliver the caution.

'The strife is o'er, the battle done.' He surprised himself by bursting out into the words of the Easter hymn. He smiled, realizing why he was feeling so pleased. Here was a case which would not end in imprisonment or real suffering for anyone. Still singing, he turned the corner into the alley.

When the ghost had vanished and the music had come to its sudden end, he had left the Archdeacon to his own devices in the Minster and quietly steered Alisdair out of the south door. Even though he knew that the ghost was a hoax, Alisdair was greatly shaken, and Septimus admitted wryly to himself that had he realized how horrific the ghost would actually look he would never have taken the boy with him. So he had seen Alisdair back to his room and safe into bed. He had turned out the light and stood watching at the window until the Archdeacon and his two helpers had come through Cloister Garth on their way home. Alisdair had already been asleep when he had climbed out of the bedroom on to the wall.

Singing his hymn Septimus walked down the alley to where it passed under the Petersteps. The street lamp on the far side of the wall was out now, but he could just see the outline of the metal ladder against the stonework. He put his hand on one of the steel rungs, tugged it experimentally, and then smoothly he climbed upward and over the coping at the top. He found himself standing in a lead-lined gutter, the slate roof of the Petersteps steep in front of him, the sheer cliff of the north wall to his right. The slates still glistened with rain, and the roof was slippery, but between wall and slates there was a broad band of lead flashing which was rough with age and easy to walk on. Septimus climbed upward until he came to the sill of the clerestory window.

Despite the risk of being seen he used his torch to find the part of the window which opened and how it was secured. There was no comment or challenge from Chandlers Way or the market-place. Probably all the reporters had phoned whatever stories they had invented to London and sensibly gone to bed. With a piece of wire, and working by feel alone, it took him about two minutes to slip the antiquated catch. A whole section of the window opened like a flap – soundlessly. No doubt it had been oiled. No doubt all the other windows in the clerestory had the same arrangement, and Septimus would have been prepared to bet a month's salary that all the others would be rusted solid.

Once inside the clerestory he used his torch again, shielding it from the window, searching the stone flags. By the door to the Lantern stairs he found what he was looking for – a patch of damp on the stone. The ghost, having climbed through the window, had stood here waiting for his cue to start the walk down the clerestory.

The question of cue was interesting. Unless there were

three people responsible for the ghost – and he was pretty sure there were only two – the cue must have worked on a time basis. You could use the music itself as a cue. Move at a predetermined moment. The rest of the music would take exactly the same time to play so you would disappear on the scream. Septimus reconstructed in his imagination the first part of the drama. The ghost had climbed through the window, put on his greatcoat and hat and waited by the door for his cue in the music. Then he had walked into the first tunnel where he had lighted his lantern. No – not lighted. There had been no flare of a match. It must be some sort of electric lantern, although it had not looked like one. Then by the light of the lantern the ghost had located the Archdeacon's first thread and stepped over it. It was curious, Septimus reflected, how the Archdeacon could happily step over his own threads without apparently considering that anyone else could do the same.

Septimus walked down the clerestory, stepping over the threads as he went, until he came to the organ. Here the ghost had waited a moment, raising the lantern to its face (how had that horrifying face been done?), then it had gone, not to the organ loft, but behind the organ. This was a point which Septimus had taken particular care to notice.

Behind the organ Septimus shone his torch up into the head of the arch, to the pulley block above the gap in the organ pipes. There was nothing over the pulley, not even a thread, but he was quite certain that there had been an hour ago – a rope stout enough to take the weight of a very material ghost. So the ghost had switched off his lantern and climbed down the rope into the lower organ chamber. Septimus went down the steps, across the nave and into the crypt, using his torch freely now. He stood in front of the partition, working out its position in relation to the Cottages in Chandlers Way. The door from the workshop – which had been a window – led into the alley. The next window must be in the store, and that would back on to Harry Tulloch's cottage. Then there would be one backing on to Ted Barnes' cottage. That one must be in the lower organ room.

The window in the store was plain to see, a round-headed shutter of plain planks in a round-headed arch. It was exactly the same as the outside entrance to the workshop, but because there were no steps below it, it was about three feet up the wall. He did not investigate it further because there was a pile of mouldering hassocks leaning against it.

In the lower organ room he found, as he expected, the same arrangement, only here there was no rubbish, just the planking three feet up the wall above the electric motor which powered the organ. All round the planking the wall was covered with cables, so many of them that they overflowed the moulding of the arch and were secured down the inside. But none of them ran across the planking itself.

The electric motor made a convenient mounting block. Septimus stood on top of it, conscious of the black rectangle above him and to his left – the hole by which the ghost had descended from the clerestory. He examined the edge of the planking with his torch. There was no sign of hinges, but the timber had been fixed on the outside of the arch, so that if it was a door the hinges would be invisible, concealed by the stone.

He pressed against the planks. They moved fractionally, like a locked door. They were firm but not solid. He set about examining the edges of the timber with minute care.

It took him five minutes to find what he was looking for – so long that he was beginning to consider the horrible possibility that he was wrong, his whole reconstruction of the haunting a fanciful piece of nonsense. But then a knot in the planking came out between his finger and thumb, and there in the cavity that it left was a keyhole.

He examined the keyhole by the light of his torch. He switched off the torch and examined the door for any trace of light from the other side. He pressed his ear to the planks and listened. There was no sign of either light or sound.

He took a bunch of skeleton keys from his pocket and set about the lock. Of course it was always possible that the door would be bolted on the inside, and that would be a pity because it would mean that he would have to go into Chandlers Way and through the front door ... And then there might be dramatic denials and hours of angry argument. It would be neater and far more dramatic if the door was only locked.

It was. After two minutes' probing Septimus felt the spring yield to his delicate touch. With his free hand he pushed against the planks and the door swung silently into darkness. He stepped up on to the sill, over and down. He shone his torch briefly around and then switched it off. He was in a tiny room, a chair in the middle of it, the rest of it full of broadcasting equipment. He stood for a full two minutes listening in the darkness. There was no indication of anyone close at hand. He turned the torch on again. He found the switch in the corner by the door and turned on the light.

The room was about six feet square. There were no windows, just two doors – the one he had entered by, a second one opposite. There were two big tape recorders, a gramophone turntable, a big control panel like something out of a broadcasting studio, and a shelf full of boxes of tape. There was a big loudspeaker in one corner and two pairs of headphones lying on a bench. He looked at the labels above the controls. 'Nave speakers . . .' numbered one to six, 'Dean's mike', 'Omni-mike', 'Organ mike'.

He studied the layout for a while. It was not entirely foreign to him because of his experiences during the War. After a while he felt confident enough to switch on the equipment. He turned up the control for the 'omni-mike'. At first there was nothing but a crackle, but then, infinitely remote, he heard the Minster clock chime the half hour. He looked at his watch. Half past one. He nodded to himself. With that microphone you would have a pretty good idea what was going on in the Minster. He turned to the boxes of tapes. There were several versions of the 'Suite for Janet' numbered from one to five. Number four, which he pulled out at random, was called, 'Suite for Janet. Full, with screams.' There were a variety of test tapes, and one labelled – intriguingly – 'Clerestory Footsteps'. On the gramophone turntable there was a copy of the 1934 recording of Primrose's Suite, and beside it there was a manuscript copy of the music with a time scale numbered in seconds in the margin.

There were two other interesting things. The first was what appeared to be one of those electric alarm clocks which make a cup of tea at a predetermined moment. The tea-making bits had been removed, and what was left was wired to one of the tape recorders. It was obviously a home-made time switch. The second was a jumble of clothing on the bench. There was a black coat, a three-cornered hat, a lantern and a woman's white nylon stocking. Septimus picked up the stocking and slipped his hand into it. It had a patterning on it so that it shimmered like shot silk in the electric light. So that was how the face had been done! He had enough experience of nylon stockings being used as masks in bank raids and wage snatches, but he guessed that this was the first one that had been used for a haunting. Next, he picked up the lantern. As he expected, it was battery-operated, but over the bulb was hung a delicate spiral of aluminium which shook and turned as you moved the lamp.

Septimus went across the little room and switched off the light. He slid his hand once again into the stocking and switched on the lantern. The coil of aluminium rocked and rotated, throwing weird shadows round the walls and across the shot silk of the stocking. The white surface looked leprous, and it seemed to heave and crawl, reminding him of the terrible face that had glared down from the clerestory. He put the stocking and the rest of the paraphernalia into the coat and rolled it all into a bundle, which he tucked under his arm. He crossed the room and pushed the door in the corner. It opened with a click and he stepped through and shone his torch around.

He was where he expected to be. In the little room containing Ted Barnes' short-wave radio. Outside the window, Harry Tulloch's back door and scullery window were blank. Evidently Harry was sensibly in bed. But nearly opposite the window, there was a crack of light beneath the door which led to the kitchen, and he could hear a murmur of voices. He moved to the door, opened it gently, and stepped softly into the lighted kitchen. There was a fire in the hearth, a meal on the table. Ted and Norman were sitting at either end of the table. In the middle of the meal was a bottle of champagne cider. Ted and Norman had their glasses raised. It was a celebration.

They were both laughing as Septimus came through the door, so that they did not hear him.

'And here's to Hezekiah Primrose,' said Ted.

'Good evening,' said Septimus.

17   Loose Ends

Ted and Norman Barnes turned as Septimus spoke from the doorway, then they froze, their glasses poised in mid-air. At last Ted stood up, slowly. He seemed neither surprised nor flustered, and there was a wry half-smile on his face. 'Evening, Mr Treloar,' he said, 'I warned Norman we might expect you. Though I didn't think you'd come from that direction.'

'You're supposed to be in Esher,' said Norman accusingly. He sounded merely irritated, not in the least apologetic.

'Can I sit down?' Septimus asked.

'Of course,' said Ted, pulling a chair out from the table. 'Have a drink, sir.'

He poured champagne cider into a glass. Septimus took the drink and looked over it at father and son. 'Hezekiah Primrose and John Jancey,' he said. He drank and put the glass down. 'Now, Ted, why did you do it?'

Ted looked down at his wine glass, toying with the stem. 'You going to tell the Dean, sir? He'll sack me for sure. Himmler'll make him.'

'That depends on why, Ted,' Septimus replied. 'But I can make no promises.'

Ted grinned suddenly, cheerfully. 'It'd be worth it – even getting sacked. Proper Charlie we've made of the Archdeacon. Spouting about the "crowning glory of his life" he was, when we came out of the Minster.'

'Says he's going to get the Dean to have the ghost laid,' said Norman.

'He'll need the Bishop for that, and holy water,' said Ted.

'But why, Ted?' Septimus asked the question gently. 'Was it because of your wife?' The laughter left Ted's mobile face, and his brown eyes were sad, remembering.

'Aye. It was because of Mary. When I knew you'd found out about Ma Wenlock, I made sure you'd find out the rest, Mr Treloar. 'Course I knew she was a fraud. But she wasn't all fraud . . .' He looked up at Septimus, a twinkle in his dark eyes. 'Just like a parson or a doctor, sir. Then that night – when Jenkins came and found the hooks and things . . . well, that night . . .' He paused, watching the bubbles rise in his glass. 'It's sad to look at her now, sir. She wasn't always like she is now. Well . . . that night she said – things. I'm not going to say what they were, not even now. Because I've never told anyone. Not even Norman. But that night Ma Wenlock said things that Mary had said on our honeymoon. No one else knew them – only Mary and me.' He stopped again, remembering. 'If I were to die tomorrow, Mr Treloar, that night my Mary spoke through Ma Wenlock. Then Jenkins came in like a great clod-hopping elephant. He smashed it all. He was so sure of himself and so bloody self-righteous.' There was a long silence in the little room.

'I see,' said Septimus at last. 'Revenge.'

'That's a hard word, Mr Treloar. "Vengeance is mine, I will repay saith the Lord." More a practical joke really. But it got out of hand.'

'I suppose it started when you helped Bert Smith with the public address system?'

Ted nodded. 'I knew Jenkins was coming, and I'd just found the door leading into my workshop. There were fifteen coats of paper over it on the inside.'

Norman took up the story.

'I'd heard the legend about Primrose from Ma Wenlock. So Dad and me, we put our heads together. Thought it would be fun to fool old Jenkins. First of all we thought we'd have some ghostly footsteps or something like that. Then Dad found the recording of the old organ in the Song School. So we settled on a ghostly organ. Didn't take much rewiring either – most of the cables run just outside the door.'

'Just what have you got out there?' asked Septimus.

Norman lit a cigarette, leaned back and blew a cloud of smoke at the light.

'There's an omni-directional mike in one of the angel's trumpets on top of the organ. Very sensitive that is. You can hear pretty well anything in the nave. It won't pick up the chapels, though. Then we can control all the speakers down the north side. Use them for a real bit of stereo sound if you want to. I wanted to run a railway engine through the nave in the middle of matins, only Dad wouldn't let me. Anyway, add tapes, a record player and a time switch, and we were pretty adaptable. Music, footsteps, screams – you name it, we could do it.'

'Norman planned it all,' said Ted. 'He's pretty good at that sort of thing.'

'I thought you worked for the Post Office,' said Septimus.

Norman smiled. 'I do. Tele-communications engineer.'

'I hoped you'd think he was a counter clerk,' said Ted. 'I did my best to throw you off the scent. How did you cotton on, sir?'

Septimus considered the question. This whole conversation was not at all like an officer-of-the-law confronting breakers of the law. But then, he wasn't an officer-of-the-law any longer, and except in a very legalistic sense indeed no laws had really been broken.

'Well there was the lantern, Ted. You couldn't have seen it from Chandlers Way . . .'

'Ah. I made a bad mistake about that. Realized it just as I was telling you that night. But I hoped I'd covered it by mucking up the recording you got of the music. I nipped down from the clerestory and ran the tape back after the music had ended.'

'It was really that that made me guess,' said Septimus. 'You see, I was certain that equipment was all right. And I was certain the music was coming out of the public address speakers because it couldn't be coming from anywhere else. So someone must have fiddled with the recorder, and the most likely person was you.'

Ted shrugged. 'Too clever by half, I am. Was there anything else?'

'Why on earth did you have to find Lovebody's Journal in the Lantern? Even the Archdeacon didn't believe that one. It was so unghostly.'

This time Ted laughed outright.

'That Journal changed the course of history as you might say. I didn't even know the details of the murder were in Lovebody's Journal until I heard Himmler sounding off to you about it in the library. So that night, I went to have a look. They'd just uncovered Primrose's coffin so I thought we might be able to bring the haunting a bit closer to what had actually happened.'

'Where were you when I came into the library?' Septimus asked.

'I was in the second cupboard, holding it shut for all I was worth. Anyway when you'd gone I scarpered with the Journal. I copied out the relevant bits, and in the morning – Wednesday that was – I took it into the Minster in my tool bag ready to put it back when I got the chance. But the librarian was there half the morning, and when he wasn't in the way Harry Tulloch was. So when you came into the Minster in the afternoon, I'd still got it in my bag. Well, I went up to the Lantern and checked it over and then I came down again ... Mr Treloar, did you notice what Harry Tulloch was carrying when you found us talking and he told you I'd found the book in the lantern?'

'No,' said Septimus, 'I don't remember.'

'Ah well, he'd got that little vacuum-cleaner he uses for the saints. Now when Harry meets me with that thing in his hand, sure as sure, the drive bands have come off and he wants to borrow tools to take it to bits. And there was me with that damn great book in my tool bag. So before he asked I told him I'd found Lovebody's Journal in the Lantern. Best I could do on the spur of the moment.'

Septimus shook his head admiringly. 'Ted, if the Dean does sack you, you could always get a job on the stage.'

'What *are* you going to tell him, Mr Treloar?' Ted was suddenly urgent.

Septimus shook his head slowly. 'I don't know yet, Ted. It's too late and I'm too tired.'

'I'm fond of the Minster. I'd be sorry to go. It was only Jenkins coming.'

Septimus passed a hand across his brow. He *was* tired, more tired than he cared to admit. He sympathized more with Ted and Norman than he did with the Archdeacon, but you really could not have vergers faking hauntings in their own cathedrals.

'Ted,' he said, 'if I managed to hush it up, this would have to be the end of hauntings – and fixing the Archdeacon.'

Father and son looked at one another. 'Yes,' said Ted.

'And will you promise to take out all that illegal wiring and burn the tapes?'

Ted nodded. 'Yes. I'll do that.'

'Fair enough. I can't promise anything, Ted. The Dean

asked me to investigate, and if he insists on knowing I'll have to tell him. But I'll do what I can.'

'Well thank you, Mr Treloar. I can't ask for fairer than that. Where are you spending the night, sir? Not under the organ I take it?'

Septimus smiled gently. 'I hadn't really thought, Ted. Actually I'm in Esher.'

'Ah well. We've got a spare room. You spend the night with us.'

'I'll lend you some pyjamas,' said Norman. He stood up and led the way to the stairs. Septimus turned at the bottom. 'One thing, Ted. I thought Norman looked a pretty horrific ghost. Scared the living daylights out of me. But why did you have to bolt out of the clerestory yourself?'

Ted laughed. 'Well, sir – which would you rather do? Bolt and pretend to Himmler that you're scared to death – or try to describe what it's like to have a ghost walk through you, when you know the ghost's your own son with a false beard and a damn silly hat like something out of *Treasure Island*?'

Once again Septimus was sitting on the wide seat in the Dean's study window. There was a bundle beside him on the seat, and he was gazing out of the window over the harbour and the sea, listening with half an ear to the Archdeacon. It was Sunday morning. He had come to the Deanery straight after the early service, but he had mistimed it. The Archdeacon was already with the Dean. Alisdair had answered the door and ushered him into the study, stopping the Archdeacon in mid-torrent. The Dean had greeted Septimus with relief, the Archdeacon with irritation and surprise.

'Treloar. So you're back. And sooner than we expected. Good news of Cowslip I trust . . .'

'Primrose,' murmured Septimus. But the Archdeacon had

not heard. He had already turned back to the Dean and resumed his relentless attack. It was all about what had happened in the Minster and what the Dean had got to do about it. Septimus let him get on with it, ignoring the mute plea in the Dean's face. Least said, soonest mended. And he certainly wasn't going to argue with the Venerable Aloysius. Life was just not long enough. And it was Sunday morning, and he was a country parson. He had managed to persuade a neighbour to take his eight o'clock service, but he had simply got to be back at Saint Mary's for eleven. Meantime, it was a lovely morning and a lovely view, Ted had given him a good breakfast ('The hangman ate a hearty breakfast,' he had said), and the Archdeacon's voice was like the background babbling of a brook – provided you didn't pay too much attention to what he was actually saying.

At last the Archdeacon appeared to be coming to an end.

'. . . and so Mr Dean, although there has clearly been some trickery, we really do face an emergence from the spirit world. Two unquiet spirits greatly in need – if I may say so – of our compassion and professional help.'

He stopped dead, obviously waiting for the Dean to agree.

The Dean said nothing for a moment and looked desperately at Septimus who seemed to be entirely engrossed in watching a herring gull circle the television aerial on top of the Archdeacon's kitchen chimney.

'M-my dear Archdeacon. What do you suggest?'

'We must get the Bishop, Mr Dean. Clearly it is a matter for the spiritual father of the diocese. After all, there is a sense in which Jancey and Primrose are his children in God – at least the children of his office, of the Bishop of this See. And you yourself, of course, as Dean of the Minster. Some time ago I devised a suitable form of service. These unhappy spirits must be set at rest, Dean. To use the common phrase, they must be laid. And it is our plain duty as the spiritual leaders of the diocese to see that it is done properly and in due order.'

'I shouldn't do that if I were you, Archdeacon,' said Septimus gently. He still appeared to be fascinated by the sea-gull.

'What do you mean, Treloar?' said the Archdeacon frostily.

Septimus stood up and turned away from the window and the two of them confronted one another down the long room; the one immaculately dressed, tall and thin, intent of face, the other big and untidy, like a retired pugilist with mild blue eyes innocent of all deception.

'If you want to lay last night's ghost, Mr Jenkins, you'll have to do it with a cosh.' He picked up the bundle from the window seat and threw it on to the table so that it unrolled, beard, hat, stocking and lantern spilling across the table. 'There's your ghost, Mr Jenkins. You see I had a look round after you'd gone last night. That's what I found.'

The Archdeacon's face was white. Septimus could not tell whether it was shock or anger.

'You found those in the Minster – last night?'

'Yes.'

'I don't believe it.'

Septimus said nothing. He just stood there looking at the Archdeacon. And to the Dean watching the two men it seemed that the Archdeacon wilted and Septimus grew in stature until he looked like a stern headmaster confronting an erring third-former.

'I-I mean . . .' The Archdeacon was hesitant, fumbling. 'How did an impostor get in? I had all the doors locked and barred. How did he get in? How did he get out?'

'In by a window over the Petersteps,' said Septimus gently. 'Out by the door from the electrician's workshop.' The lie was justifiable and he told it unblushingly.

'But what about my tell-tale threads?'

'If you can step over them, Archdeacon, so can a ghost.'

'You mean some imposter ... some ... some rogue ...'
The Archdeacon had by now climbed back on to his usual
clerical perch, and he was furious.

'You mean someone like, like one of those journalists . . .?'
He got no further.

'Oh, my God!' said Septimus and without explanation he
ran out of the study and out of the Deanery, leaving the
front door swinging behind him. John Jones of the *Advertiser* was still in the coke-hole.

Harry Tulloch was standing by the coke-hole door. Re-
splendent in his Sunday cassock and gown he was leaning
with one hand on the buttress and carrying on a conversation through the planks.

'Well if Mr Treloar locked you in there it serves you
bloomin' well right. And you can starve to death for all I
care.'

Together Septimus and Harry unbolted the door and Mr
Jones emerged, blinking owlishly in the sunlight. He was
very angry and swore shockingly at Septimus.

'Tut, tut!' said Harry. 'Language! On the Sabbath and all.
You'll have a gargoyle fall on your head, you will.'

Septimus could not take Mr Jones's wrath seriously. He
had been sworn at far too many times before. And anyway,
Mr Jones looked so extraordinary. Like a refugee from the
Black and White Minstrels, Septimus decided – except that
his suit was the same colour as his face.

'And what about the story you promised me?' shouted Mr
Jones. He dragged out a handkerchief – dazzling white
against the prevailing gloom – and started to mop his face.
This only made matters worse.

'Yes. The story,' Septimus muttered. 'As a matter of fact
the Dean and I were just in the middle of making it up when

I suddenly remembered you. So you can go home and wash your face, Mr Jones, and put on a nice clean suit, and call on the Dean in the morning. And don't go falling into any more coke-holes.' He turned back to the Deanery.

'You horrible parson! I hate you,' shouted John Jones at the retreating back.

'Watch it, mate,' said Harry equably. 'Don't niggle the Major – unless you want to become the Ghost of the Coke-Hole Reporter. And we can't do with another haunting, as the actress said to the bishop.'

The Archdeacon had gone when Septimus got back to the Dean's study. The Dean made him sit down. 'Now the f-fury and the shouting have departed, you can tell me all about it, my dear Septimus.' Septimus looked up into the other man's gentle, ascetic face.

'I'd rather not, sir,' he said. 'I don't want to tell you all about it, because it might involve you in action you wouldn't want to take.'

'My dear man,' said the Dean. 'Tell me as much as you want to, then.'

Septimus gave a brief account of the affair, leaving out all the details that implicated Ted Barnes, and telling downright lies when necessary.

'That's as near the truth as I want to tell you sir,' he ended. 'I'll tell you the rest if you insist. But I'd rather not.'

The Dean was silent for a long time. And then, 'What was the motive?' he asked gently.

'A practical joke, really. Someone who wanted to make the Archdeacon look a fool.'

'And did he deserve it – the Archdeacon?'

Septimus thought of Ted and his sad little story about his wife.

'Yes,' he said with violence, 'yes. He did deserve it. Of course he never meant to do any harm, but people without a sense of humour are too dangerous to be on the loose. If it had been me . . . I don't think I'd have played a joke on him. I'd have committed g.b.h. Clobbered him with a blunt instrument.'

'I see,' said the Dean. He went to the window and stood there looking out.

'And it's all over now? No more weird music? No more ghosts? No more journalists?' he spoke without turning.

'It's all over,' said Septimus. 'My promise. And the ghost's promise.'

The Dean turned and smiled. 'I think we can leave it at that, my dear Septimus. And I can't thank you enough, and certainly not now because I've got to get ready for matins, but . . .'

'Oh, my God!' said Septimus for the second time that morning. 'Matins! Time I wasn't here. I've got to get back to Danedyke. I'll have to drive like the clappers. See you in court, Dean.' He bolted, slamming the door behind him this time.

The Dean looked at the blank white panels for a moment, and then a long slow smile lit up his face. 'Bless the man,' he said. 'He is given to dramatic entrances and exits.'

Alisdair, who had been lurking in the hall since he finished his breakfast, chased Septimus out of the Deanery.

'Hey! Septimus.'

'Can't stop now! I'm due in church.' He was pounding through the Peterport.

'All right. I'll come with you.'

There was no chance for conversation as they ran down Chandlers Way, and when they tumbled into the car they were both too breathless, so that it was some minutes before they could talk.

Septimus drove carefully out of the town and then accelerated to top speed and went snarling along the straight fen roads. Alisdair, his lank hair whipping like flags, turned to this big priest who was also his friend. He had to shout to make his voice audible above the wind.

'So it's all over?'

Septimus nodded without taking his eyes off the road.

'And who did it, Holmes?' Septimus took his foot off the accelerator and changed down for the sharp bridge across the Danedyke. As his left hand came off the gear lever he grabbed Alisdair's floppy hair and shook it affectionately, before bringing his hand smoothly back to the wheel.

'I didn't tell your father, Watson, and I'm not telling you. So that's one story you'll never write. But thanks for your help.'

The car climbed gently on to the hump of the bridge, and from far behind them over the fen they could both hear the gay bells of Minster Saint Peter.

About the Author

Stephen Chance's roots are firmly planted in East Anglia. Both his father and mother were born in Peterborough, and he remembers with great affection holidays spent exploring the remote villages of the fen country, with their strong-walled cottages and thatched roofs, the dykes and the cathedral-like parish churches (one of which was surely the model for St Mary's Danedyke).

Trained as a mechanical engineer at the end of what he describes as 'an undistinguished war', Stephen Chance soon forsook engineering for a variety of other jobs which have included work in H.M. prisons, youth work and hospital administration. He has always been fascinated by the buildings and clergy of the Church of England, not so much as an expression of Christian faith but as an aspect of English history.

Stephen Chance is married and has two teenage sons.